Metaphorosis

March 2018

Beautifully made speculative fiction

Also from Metaphorosis Books

Reading 5X5: Readers' Edition
Reading 5X5: Writers' Edition

Best Vegan Science Fiction & Fantasy

Best Vegan SFF of 2017
Best Vegan SFF of 2016

Metaphorosis Magazine

Metaphorosis: Best of 2017
Metaphorosis: Best of 2016
Metaphorosis 2017: The Complete stories
Metaphorosis 2016: Nearly Complete Stories
Monthly issues

by B. Morris Allen

Susurrus
Allenthology: Volume I
Tocsin: and other stories
Start with Stones: collected stories
Metaphorosis: a collection of stories

Metaphorosis

March 2018

edited by
B. Morris Allen

Metaphorosis Books

Neskowin

ISSN: 2573-136X (online)
ISBN: 978-1-64076-102-5 (e-book)
ISBN: 978-1-64076-105-6 (paperback)

March 2018

Always Dawn to Forever Night.................7
by Luke Elliott

Any Old Disease....................................27
by Dimitra Nikolaidou

Velaya, the Dreaming City.....................63
by Beston Barnett

Switch...105
by Lisa Clark

The Three Sisters................................163
by Keith Azariah-Kribbs

Always Dawn to Forever Night

Luke Elliott

Pwela woke to a chill unknown in the Forest of Always Dawn. Tar and peat filled the air, undercutting the perpetual crispness. She shot to her bare feet.

While she slept, the Rot Thing had stolen her warmstone.

Her warmstone sustained her, let her live in the everglow of the forest. Her palms went slick and her breath came short and shallow. She should flee. Run as far and fast as skylight arcing over a cloud. She should, but she would not. She hated the Rot Thing. It had brought unwelcome change to the Continuance.

She could not allow it. She would reclaim her warmstone.

Pwela found Loper resting in a glade of white heather and woke him with a whistle.

"What is it?" he said, jaws cracking with his yawn. The bogcat stretched his long black body, first his back legs, then his front. Extended claws raked the heather, upturning black loam, and a long tail swished high in the air.

"The Rot Thing stole my warmstone."

Loper hissed.

"You smell it, too. Tar and peat." She scratched behind one of his long, feathered ears in the way he liked. She laid her head against his neck, his ghost-striped fur smooth against her bare scalp. "Will you take me after it?"

"Only since it's you asking," he said.

Such a softie. She climbed onto his back, settling between bony spines.

Loper carried her through the Forest of Always Dawn. The orange of the low-roosting sun lit the leaves in its unending glow, dappling the forest floor. Loper darted into the underbrush, then leapt out onto a fir. Long claws sank into its mossy trunk as he bounded off, clearing a sinkhole full of vine snarls. Pwela held fast to the mane of black hair around his neck, her skin blending against his fur. The harmony of their colors was music.

She laughed as they soared, eyes leaking.

Another leap took them into the heart of a familiar glen. But where baby's breath once flourished white and pink, stains now colored flowers with yellow and brown. Wilting from the Rot Thing's passing.

"What is it?" she asked. But she knew.

Loper bent to chew the grass, then spat with a hacking cough. He growled, a rumbly sound from deep within his chest. "Wrongness stains our forest, Pwela."

She sat tall on Loper's back. "The Rot Thing carries stain and wilt and canker. We must drive it out."

"Do you know the Rot Thing?" her friend asked, voice a near-whisper.

She had never met it, but found she did know. "I have long dreamt of it." A shiver shook her small frame.

"As have I," Loper said.

Together, they followed a trail of wrongness in pursuit of the Rot Thing. The thick underbrush and wide trees of the Forest of Always Dawn thinned and lapsed away. Lessening was the way of borders, but swathes of ugly wrongness marred the gentle margins. It hurt her chest to see beauty so wronged.

And so they crossed into the Desert of Only Day. The sun shone savage above, its radiance afire atop the sands.

"The Rot Thing walks the desert," said Loper. "I smell its wrongness, tar and peat." He climbed a dune slowly, paws sinking.

"Shall I walk?"

"The sand is fire, Pwela. Your softness would not long last it." The heat already lashed against her scalp. Oddly, though, a chill remained in her belly.

"You are kind to worry." She let one hand free of his mane to scratch at a long, feathered ear. "But if you tire, my softness will manage." Bogcats were not of the desert. They came from the deep Moor of Forever Night, where they hunted through chill and gloom. Loper had only come to live in the Forest of Always Dawn to be with her, though he grew to love it.

Loper plodded on, persisting against his disharmony with the desert. If he could endure such extremes, she too could reach the gateway, where surely the Rot Thing headed. Its path was no mystery to her, she realized, and that unsettled her stomach. Perhaps she would even discover what lay beyond the gate. Thoughts of what lay beyond filled her with anxiety, a shrill thing. It made her all out of tune.

An immense dune rose above the rolling sands, so tall it brushed the sun. Its sands quivered and roiled.

"What is it?" she said, gasping.

Loper paused. His back hair bristled against her skin. "Come out," he yelled. The bogcat stepped closer to the dune, growling. His ropy muscles coiled beneath her thighs. "You who lurk beneath the sands, come topside."

The dune rippled, and two long eyestalks burst skyward. Each eyestalk reached higher than Pwela would if she stood on Loper's back. Black orbs swelled at their ends.

A voice like an avalanche shook beneath them. "How dare you tread upon our sands, bogcat? And with that wretched manthing clinging to your fur?"

"I tread where I wish, prawn," said proud Loper.

The eyestalks rose higher and an immense horned shell clove the sands. Chitinous legs tipped with forked pincers lifted a carapace half out. Thick antennae whipped the sands, sending Loper back on his haunches. Fetid winds eddied around the creature.

Pwela stifled a gasp.

"We are not prawn." The voice fell over them.

The dune devil was the largest she'd ever seen, perhaps the largest in all the Continuance.

"I am this bogcat's friend, Old One," Pwela said. "Forgive him, please. He can be thorny for a feline."

"Why does the manthing make words at us?"

Loper growled, prowling the sands.

"I am Pwela. I would be your friend as well."

The dune devil's antennae ceased their lashing.

Pwela unslung herself from Loper's back. Her breath hissed at the burning of the desert. The softness of her feet indeed hated the fiery sand. She trudged toward the dune devil, palms raised. "We only seek to cross your dunes and enter the meadow. We chase the Rot Thing."

"Rot Thing?" the old devil demanded. "You are with the Rot Thing?" An enormous claw rose from the sands around Pwela and clamped over her chest. The dune devil drove out her wind. She gasped, fighting for air.

Loper snarled. "Release her, you crusty shrimp."

The dune devil lifted her toward its maw. Hot, dry breath reeking of spoiled fish blasted her from the furnace of the devil's gullet. Arm-like mandibles grasped for her.

"We are not with the Rot Thing," she screamed. "Enemies, enemies!"

The dune devil stopped just shy of biting into her. "We hate the Rot Thing," it said, voice all clacks and clicking. "Look what it did to us." The dune devil rolled onto one side and moved her toward its underbelly. Black stains of ichor marred its orange carapace. The pools spread inky tendrils, even as she watched.

"It's horrible," she said, eyes welling. Dull ache filled her own belly, chilled from within.

The dune devil released her. Before the sands burned her softness, Loper was at her side, head dipped so she could clamber on to his back.

"How do we beat the Rot Thing, old one?" she asked. "How can I save you from its wrongness and destroy it?"

"You cannot," said the dune devil. It quivered, slowly descending back into the sands. "The Rot Thing has always been, though it shifts form."

"I must try," she said, lip thrust out. "I will reclaim my warmstone and not allow wrongness to desolate my Continuance."

"The Continuance is not yours, manthing," said the dune devil. Soon, only its eyestalks remained above the sands. "It is not for belonging. Shared by all and none."

"Once I cast out the Rot Thing, will you heal?" she asked.

"Look to yourself," the dune devil said. Its eyestalks dipped beneath the sands, which stilled as if nothing had ever lurked beneath its shifting layers.

"We must go, Pwela," said Loper. "Even I cannot long withstand the fire." And go they did, across the Desert of Only Day's long reaches, until tufts of sawgrass dotted sand that lapsed into soil. The sun dipped in the crossing, turned purple.

They entered the gentle meadow of the Everdusk.

Though Pwela was most comfortable in the Forest of Always Dawn, she adored the Everdusk. She and Loper had come once before, played on beds of lilac, rolled together beneath the tranquil light. The autumn wind blew songs of sleepiness and slow. The meadow was a place for resting.

But wrongness had come to the Everdusk, too. The lilac sea had wilted, petal clusters browned and decayed. A sign of the Rot Thing's passing.

The path wound down into the moor and out of sight. Her feet tried to follow, but she forced them to halt. She felt the end in her belly, and rested her palm over the chill. The path led, eventually, to the gate.

"What ails you?" Loper asked.

"A chill," Pwela said, peering at her stomach. She gasped. Wrongness marred her as well, spread from her belly in tendrils of sick.

Loper could not see her belly, since she still rode astride his back. "What is it?" he asked.

"I need my warmstone," she said. "The chill runs deep now, and I cannot shake it." She would spare him the truth.

"We should turn back," said Loper. His black paws sank into the wilted sea. "Please, Pwela. No joy or beauty lies ahead."

"I must face it," she whispered. "It has my warmstone, and without it I cannot stay here. You can go back. Return to the Forest of Always Dawn and run among the elm and fir."

"No." Loper flattened his long ears. "I shall carry you all the way."

She scratched those ears while they walked the lilac sea, which shimmered with light and wind, but soon, far too soon, the meadow, too, began to lapse. The purple glow darkened, deepened, until only black remained. A crescent moon hung alone in the sky at the edge of the Moor of Forever Night, shining pale like milk, white like bone. The dying lilacs turned to weeds and snarls and damp.

She had never been so far.

The blackness of Forever Night had haunted her dreams as long as she could remember, beckoning her. It had been the Rot Thing all along, she realized, summoning her to the gate.

Loper sloshed through puddles as dark as his fur, between the shadows of cypress trees like grasping ghouls. The moor was his home, she reminded herself. Bogcats lived in harmony with the darkness at the heart of the Continuance, prowled the paths surrounding the gateway. Loper would protect her.

The swamp stank of tar and peat. Loper raised his head to sniff the air, then bounded forward through the gloom. Eyes glinted back through shadow, reflecting moonlight. Loper did not slow, for his eyes glinted too, and the unseen things did not assail them.

They emerged, at last, onto the bank of a still lake lit only by the crescent moon which dipped low over the water, as if reaching for its own reflection. At the middle of the lake rose an island of pale sand. At its center lay the freestanding gateway, plain and brown, locked and bolted.

As it should be.

But beside it stood a figure dark beyond mere black. It stung her eyes like an inverse sun. The Rot Thing. On the island, the Rot Thing extended white hands holding a shape red and luminous, light stark against its depth of black.

Her warmstone.

The Rot Thing lifted the red rock high and brought it down upon the gateway with a crack that thundered over the still lake, raising low ripples. The gate shook and shuddered.

Loper whimpered. "Turn back, Pwela. I cannot swim."

She climbed off his back. "I know. But you have carried me far. And I *can* swim. Stay here, my friend. I will face it alone. Someone must." Her heart told her so. "Let it be me."

"I... understand." Loper said, dipping his wide head. "Our moments in the forest live eternal, though we've passed them by. I am with you, whether you sense me or not. And if you return, I will find you again on the shore."

Pwela hugged his neck, eyes leaking, then dove into the still waters, breaking them, casting waves across the lake. Cold beyond ice bit her everywhere, though not as cold as the wrongness in her belly, but soon the pain of the chill lapsed too. She swam, arm over arm, legs pumping. She laughed as she sped toward the island, laughed despite it all. The song of the water played in her heart, filling her. When she reached the island, she climbed out, cold and dripping, but full of harmony.

"Let the gateway be," she commanded. "It must remain shut."

The Rot Thing stood with its back to her, hood drawn, looming over the gateway, its huge umbral mass shifting and fluid. It smashed the warmstone against the gateway again with a thunder that forced Pwela to cover her ears. Her red rock broke. The gateway's frame cracked, and the Rot Thing turned, then dropped the shining shards of her warmstone to the pale sand. It returned its long hands to its sides.

"No!" she cried. She dropped to her knees and cupped the fragments. Their light faded and was gone.

She dropped the broken bits and glared at the Rot Thing. Her eyes stung from gazing upon shadow so deep, but they soon adjusted too, even to blinding oblivion. She did not look away.

"You do not belong," she said. "Leave this place and never return."

"None belong. All belong," it said, throwing back its hood. "Look within and know you brought me here." The Rot Thing's voice came as a hollow echo of her own, rebounding from an endless cavern. The head of the Rot Thing was her own bald head, but distorted and immense.

Chill radiated from it, sapping her strength. She wanted to scream, to run as far and fast as skylight. She should flee, but she did not.

"You cannot trick me, bastard," she said, rising from the sand. "I did not bring you. You are *not* welcome here. Leave this place!" She set her feet wide and lifted her fists.

"There is only one way." It laid a thin hand against the gateway. "Join me." The Rot Thing's immense face was like her own, but wrongness filled empty eyes above lips blue and frigid.

The gateway opened, and nothing lay beyond. An abyss with no color at all.

She should have never come. The Forest of Always Dawn waited still. Stained though it was, at least it held warmth and sun.

A place for beginnings, not ends.

But no, the wrongness had spread through the heather, through the fir and lilac. To herself.

The Rot Thing held out its hand to her, fingers like white worms.

She searched the far bank for Loper, but the bogcat had gone. It did not anger her. Such things were not easy to witness.

The Rot Thing waited, hand extended.

"I will not go with you," she said, but did not shrink away from the awful hand.

"You will," it said, voice still a hollow echo of her own. "I will not tell you to be unafraid. I will not barter or beg. But you will come."

She stared at the nothing beyond the gate. "What is it? Is there something farther in I cannot see?"

The Rot Thing stood silent, spindle fingers swaying before her. The only way to know was to step through.

She thought of the wilted heather, the browning lilac, the wheezing old dune devil. Loper, so worried for her softness, who had carried her over fire.

"Will you leave the Continuance if I go with you?" she

said.

It paused, silent for a time before responding. "I came for you."

Then it was right. "I'm sorry, Loper," she whispered.

She took its hand. Her tiny fingers stuck to the Rot Thing's pallid skin as if it were tar. Near translucent skin. She gasped as black eels wriggled beneath the thin membrane of its being. They coiled beneath her hand, drawn to her warmth.

The crescent moon rent and tumbled from the black. The still lake spilled skyward, rising in a geyser around her.

With one long hand, the Rot Thing pushed through the absence of the gateway and pulled her through with the other, away from the Continuance. She could not stay, only go. And go, she did. Through and beyond into nowhere.

About the story

To tell the story behind "Always Dawn to Forever Night," I need to first share some tragic personal history. My mother died from stage IV brain cancer in 2012 after battling the disease for years exceeding her prognosis. Her passing left me numb as conflicting emotions fought each other once her ordeal was over. I never really dealt with the pain and injustice. I just tried the best I could to carry on.

Then, in 2015, my German-shepherd mix died unexpectedly while in the care of a vet for a minor issue. She was 3 years old. I'd adopted the dog before my mother's death and she had helped me cope when it happened, with her unconditional love. I blamed myself for her death (though I'd done nothing wrong). All the unresolved pain rushed back, combining with the guilt to overwhelm me, and sent me into a depression lasting months.

One night during that depression I dreamt about a young girl who lived on a world where the time of day was linked to geographical location. Only through travel could she witness the passage of time. Her journey began in a warm forest of perpetual dawn and ended in a land of night filled with foreboding. As she drew closer to the end, she became frightened, but continued. The dream ended abruptly without a satisfying conclusion when I woke. The concept of her world stayed with me even as details of the dream faded, so I typed a note in my phone about the potential story idea.

My waking mind connected the dream to the journey of our lives. How we begin young and worry-free and travel toward our twilight years with growing anxiety about what lies beyond. I realized what I'd dreamt was my subconscious trying to grapple with mortality. I didn't know who the girl was, but I sensed that even though she was afraid, she was brave, and willing to face whatever waited for her. The characters of Loper and the Rot Thing took shape as I crafted a story out of the building blocks my subconscious provided.

I wrote the first draft in one sitting and by the end felt euphoric and proud. Still, I'm savvy enough to know that just because you're drunk on a draft doesn't mean the story is good, so I let it sit. My suspicions were right. It needed a lot of work, but its heart was compelling. I rewrote it several times before showing it to my wife, who cried when she read it. Next, I sent it to critique partners, who helped shape it, before the final product was ready to query.

"Always Dawn to Forever Night" represents much I can't put into words about death and my admiration for people brave enough to face it with dignity. Several readers have asked what happens next and I always smile, because the answer haunts me as well.

A question for the author

Q: What do you think is the single most important quality for a good writer to possess?

A: Persistence. There will be days you want to quit. There will be months where you feel like all you are doing is banging your head against the keyboard and producing nothing remotely readable. You will get rejections. Oh, so many rejections. Saying "persistence" might be trite, but as long as you continue to learn and grow, it's the path to success.

About the author

Luke Elliott was born and raised in the suburbs of central Florida. In his late twenties, he travelled across the country with his wife and two dogs to live in Portland, Oregon, where he fell in love with the city and a region with natural beauty as magical as any fantasy world. He has a B.A. in Creative Writing from the University of Florida where he studied and wrote both literature and poetry, and earned a MFA in

Writing Popular Fiction from Seton Hill University. Now he writes mostly science fiction, fantasy, and horror, but will go wherever inspiration leads. In August of 2017, he launched the *Ink to Film* podcast with a filmmaker co-host, where he discusses books and their film adaptations from a writer's point of view. In between writing and podcasting, he collects quality single malts and is always happy to pour a dram for company.

www.lukeelliottauthor.com, @luminousluke

Any Old Disease

Dimitra Nikolaidou

"What is *wrong* with him?"

Ada had heard that tone before, the horror of a newly assigned doctor witnessing the Leak for the first time. She waited for the novice's breath to settle.

"He is withering," she said, her gaze fixed upon the man slowly expiring in front of them, his eyes already blinded, his skin paper-thin and stained. "For years on end, he is going to waste away; his remaining senses will dull, his organs will fail and in the end, he will die. This is what doctors here refer to as the Leak. As for what exactly is wrong with him, what the causes are and how it can be stopped

— well, this is exactly what we are trying to figure out here, in this Institute. This is why we need you." She let that sink in. This was the make-or-break moment, when someone decided whether they had the stomach to stay and deal with the horror on a daily basis, or walked away and drank themselves to oblivion.

The younger woman crossed her arms in front of her, eyes still fixed on the man beyond the glass. So far, she seemed to take it in better than Ada herself had, so many years ago.

"I will do everything I can to find a cure for this disease," the woman said in the end, and Ada let go of a breath she had not realized she was holding. She had liked this one from the start; it would have been a pity to see her go the way of so many others.

The novice's name was Cybele and now that she had made up her mind to stay, Ada could finally allow herself to get to know her. The two of them rode the glass elevator that went all the way up to the Institute's terrace in silence, emerging as the sun's last rays bled over the snow-covered mountains.

The view was sublime as always, yet it failed to draw a reaction out of the Cybele; she kept staring at her drink instead.

"It gets better," Ada said, after a few moments of silence.

Cybele glanced at her, lips parted, and then turned back to her cup. The signs

of shock were still etched on her face; the sun-tanned skin was now cast in grey, and her green eyes, so bright and curious this morning, had retreated into their sockets.

Ada said no more, let the woman compose her thoughts in peace. To see patients dying of the Leak took the wind out of your lungs; it was not so much the physical decay, the so very slowly crumbling skin, the hair turning to ash. No disease was a pleasant sight, after all. No, there was something else about the Leak, something visceral, whispering threats under your skin, pulling you when common sense told you to run. But then again, common sense was not the strong suit of anyone working at the Institute.

"I apologize." Cybele said eventually. "I thought I was prepared."

"This isn't any old disease. It has that effect on everyone who encounters it. Take your time."

Cybele nodded. Her eyes seemed to take in the landscape around them before settling back on Ada.

"Do they understand what's happening to them?"

"They understand everything at first. Yet by the end, even the mind is gone." Some considered this a blessing. Ada did not.

"Why is this disease so little known outside the Institute?" Cybele asked. "I tried to read up on it before coming up here but there's very little out there. Just a few vague footnotes, and an ancient, inconclusive case study."

Ada shrugged. "Well, this is the rarest of diseases. No known cause, no cure. Every single case is brought to us, and since we still do not know how it spreads, we have chosen to remain as isolated as we can. Plus, for now, we do not want to publish our findings."

"Why not?"

"Institute's policy. As obscure as a black cat's soul."

For the first time after witnessing the Leak, Cybele's eyes came back to focus.

"But then, where do the Institute's funds come from? This facility looks anything but cheap."

Ada lifted the cup to her lips. "The Director scored us a government contract, untold eons ago. It means we're under the Health Ministry's thumb, but it's a relief to actually work instead of hunting down funds every second semester."

Cybele did not speak for a moment, then mimicked Ada's shrug. She settled on her chair a little better. "And this?" she asked, looking at Ada's glossy chrome and matte carbon-fiber left hand. "Did you get it working here?"

"This? No... no." Ada clenched the metal fingers, then left them immobile again. "It was a landmine in New Paris." She held the hand up and the fingers caught the last flashes of the setting sun, silver painted molten red. "I can't be a surgeon anymore of course, but it beats a pirate's hook."

Cybele laughed, and Ada smiled back. The memory always summoned pinpricks of fire on her skin, but she sensed the unspoken questions in the air and pressed on.

"We were a bunch of volunteers from the medical faculty, searching for survivors in the ruins. We had gone as far as the Louvre crater, and were looking for a way to pass through when our guide slipped and landed face down on the wrong side of a minefield."

This was as much as she could say for now — perhaps in a few hundred years she would be able to talk about the rest, about flying deafened through the debris and the flame, about landing on her best friend's body, about Milo and Anwuli pulling her away seconds before the collapse, or about or any of the things that came after. For the time being, she just took another gulp.

"Prosthetics are the reason I decided to go into medicine," Cybele said, shifting the subject. Empathy; a useful trait in a doctor. "Everyone else thought I was destined to be a historian, or a journalist. Something with digging up the past, anyway. The world had 10 billion people before the Great Floods, and all their stories are now lost; someone has to find them, and I wanted it to be me. However, in the end I found myself so touched by the engineering feats of prosthetists, that I knew I had to be a part of it."

"Prosthetics don't do anything for them, you know," Ada said, nodding towards the underground labs where the Leak drained their patients away. "Nothing does."

"And they just wither away like that? Till they are gone?"

Ada nodded. "You will get attached to your first. I won't say don't do it; we all did."

Cybele didn't answer. She took another sip, lips tight, fingers tense. She seemed secretive, but it mattered little. Isolated as they were up in the mountain, miles away from any village, everyone opened up eventually, and let go.

After all, they had all the time in the world.

The Institute was a pile of glass boxes, panels, and domes, designed to let as much light as possible slip in through the day. The Leaks, however, were secured underground; they were too fragile, and always cold. As a result, Ada had to spend half her day below the frozen earth with them and at the end of her every shift, no matter how sharp the alpine cold was, she always needed to go outside the crystal walls even for a minute, in order to start breathing again.

"How is the novice doing?"

Milo asked the question as soon as the elevator started moving towards the terrace. In the six months that had passed since she and Cybele had shared their first coffee up there, the days had become much shorter. The sun had already set when they stepped out, but the view remained magnificent; starlight reflected on sculpted snow.

"Better than most," Ada said. The elevator doors closed behind them without a sound and they both let a few moments pass, bathing in the night. So far up the mountains there was almost no wildlife to break the silence —just their own long exhalations, carrying away the day. "She caught up fast, doesn't flinch near the Leaks, even asked a couple of questions that got me thinking."

Milo let a half-laugh out. "Doesn't flinch? Are you sure she's human?"

"Shut up." She just looked at the snow for a moment, half a word riding on each breath but none getting out of her lips. "I wish I knew how she does it. It is getting in the way of our research, the way the disease freaks out the rest of us."

"I know. I know." Levity had been chased away from his tone now. "Hey, if she can do what we can't, we are lucky to have her here. Just... don't blame yourself for not being her."

Her anger evaporated and she sighed. "I know. She just reminded me why I signed up for this in the first place. She cares for them the way I used to care when I first came here – nowadays, I feel I'm just continuing the work out of stubbornness."

"It takes all kinds. The compassionate, the stubborn, the morbidly fascinated and even those of us trapped up here by our bloody contract." He closed his eyes and stretched, head to toe. "Not that I do not share your frustration. Sometimes, for all our hard work, I swear we are just going in circles."

"True." They weren't supposed to talk about work after their shift had ended; eight hours with the Leaks were draining enough. Some days, though, were more intense than others and today, their oldest patient had refused to continue treatment. It would be a matter of days before her clouded eyes closed out the world for good –her life seeping towards the darkness in the center of the earth.

The words snuck out of Ada's mouth. "What if... what if we aren't meant to find the truth?"

"What?"

"Come on. We've circled the issue before, let us say it out loud. There are files missing from the Institute's research. You can tell by the serial numbers. Most of it is older work, but still. Why lock away anything at all, if we 're so desperate for answers?"

Milo looked at her. For a moment, the stars did not blink.

"Are you the one who put Cybele up to it, then?" he asked.

"Up to what?"

"Snooping. Asking to cross-reference old research. Was it you?"

"What? Of course not. When did that happen? And why would I set a newcomer to do my snooping for me? I've been here for ever."

"I'm sorry." He ran his hand through his hair. "You've wondered aloud about the missing files so many times in the past, and the Director never reacts well to the implication, so..."

She waited, but Milo had stopped talking. "So you thought I conned the rookie into asking on my behalf," she said, arms crossed.

"Hey, I would've done it if I were you. Anything to avoid his stare. Noticed how he started locking his office door a month ago? How he revoked half our access codes for no reason? I think he hired extra guards a week ago; some of the faces outside the fence are new. He's getting more paranoid by the day."

Ada had noticed, but she was still pissed at Milo, and chose to leave all his words unanswered.

Three months after that spat, spring rode over the mountain top. Now the third floor cafeteria was always full early in the mornings; nobody wanted to lose a moment of sunlight before heading underground to work. She braced herself for the cheerfulness, but the minute she walked in, everyone stopped talking for the briefest of moments, and then resumed chattering with half an eye turned towards her.

Milo was the only one to keep his eyes on her; she moved towards his table, but then he nodded imperceptibly towards the windows. With one last glance at him, she walked up to the glass, and looked outside.

The sun was melting the scarce snow they had gotten last night, and Cybele was out there, holding the last flakes in her hands. Showing them to a Leak.

Ada sighed on the inside. The new ones always got attached, and then did something stupid about it. The Leaks — *the patients* — were exactly as fragile as they looked. Taking them out of the underground bunker was not doing them any favors. This one seemed so far down the road, that even talking in the chilly air burdened his lungs. On the other hand, they all had done something like that when they were as fresh as Cybele was. Ada would have a talk with her later on.

Ada turned away, only to find herself almost stepping on the Director's toes.

It took her a few more seconds to realize that the cafeteria had fallen silent, everyone staring in their cups, ears cocked to her side.

"Look at her," the Director said, through a mirthless smile. He was a head taller than her, and made of slippery ice. "Brave, isn't she?"

Ada did not answer. Cybele looked up. The Director did not acknowledge her; he brought his cup to his lips but did not drink. Cybele turned to her patient again, as if he were the only person in the world.

Around them, snow began falling again.

"How do you do this?"

"Do what?" Cybele was several steps ahead as they climbed down the snow-dusted slope, but she stopped and turned.

"Be so comfortable around them." Cybele remained silent, and eventually Ada caught up to her. They stared at the distance for a while. Below them, whiffs of clouds concealed the valley at the feet of the mountains. The pyramidal tip of an old church steeple, probably buried under the ground three thousand years ago, when the Great Floods had covered the old world in water, was the only landmark as far as their eyes could see.

"I don't know," Cybele said at the end. "Why not? In the end, it is just another disease. You get used to the symptoms and proceed to the treatment."

"I know. But for most of us, it took much, much longer."

"So everyone keeps telling me. Sometimes, I think I freak you out as much as the patients do."

"True," Ada said. Cybele looked up at her in surprise; the older woman simply shrugged. It took a few more seconds before they both burst out laughing. "You do score points for constantly aggravating the Director, however."

"Not my intention," said Cybele, and her tone made Ada hold her next words back. Just mentioning the man's name seemed to cast a shadow these days, and the mountain light was receding too fast for comfort anyway.

"So where are you from? I never asked" she said instead, kicking a stone down the slope. It did not even echo as it rolled.

"Northern Greece. The great wind farms. Ever been there?"

"No. Not yet. Perhaps when I am done with the Institute."

"You have a bucket list for afterwards?"

"Not really. Who knows what I will want to do when I'm finished here. Probably just fish in the sun for the next thirty years. Not that my contract expires any time soon."

"Has anyone ever left?"

Ada hesitated. It sounded too sinister to say it out loud that no, nobody ever had. There was work to be done, still, and after so long, the outside seemed distant and noisy. Cybele stared at her a few seconds more, and then turned back to look at the setting sun being impaled on the solitary church steeple.

"Come on, let's walk a bit more" she said. "We don't have much time left."

Shots woke Ada up in the night.

Her eyes opened. She should be startled, should maybe even panic as the dry sounds tore the air. As she reached for the light, though, she realized she had been half-waiting for something big to happen, ever since Cybele had taken the patient out in the snow half a year ago. When you live so long in a place, you can read the change in the air.

There was no alarm going off, no red lights blinking. If she hadn't heard shots before, she might even write the sound off as a distant avalanche and go back to sleep. However, this was not a choice now. She got up, found her morning clothes

and slipped her white coat over them—
the most useless armor ever.

She cracked her door open and looked
across the corridor, at Cybele's room.

The door was half open, and no-one
was inside. No laptop on the desk either.

She was preparing to go over when an
armed man in black uniform turned the
corner. Her heart clenched; the Institute
guards did not carry weapons and they
had never stepped inside the main
building, for as long as she had worked
there. This man was military; an outsider.

"Are you all right, Doctor?" he asked,
cold in his tracks.

"What is going on?"

"You are not to worry. Please return to
your room."

"I need to check on my patients."
Cybele was closer to them than to her
colleagues; perhaps Ada would find some
kind of answer in their quarters. The man
was not actively stopping her, but there is
a thing about guns, they talk in a way
mouths can't. "Getting them upset is not
good, for any one."

Yes, he had his guns — but she could
always rely on the terrifying aura of the
Leak.

It worked. "All right, Doctor. You can go down, but I will need to escort you."

She nodded and walked to the underground entrance, the guard one step behind her, his boots leaving muddied prints on the pristine floor. She had hoped to get rid of him once they reached the basement but of course, no such luck. The accordion doors parted for them, and they entered the underground.

He gasped at the sight of the Leaks behind the glass walls; his sudden shock would be her only chance. She ducked into one of the glass rooms fast, and closed the door before he could gather up the courage to follow. It locked behind her, and she hoped the man would not know how much she was going against the rules by doing this.

She knelt by the bed, and whispered to the patient under the covers. "I'm Cybele's friend. I need to help her. Please, if you do know, tell me what's going on. Is she safe?"

The man was one of their oldest patients; his hair had fallen off long ago and his skin was stained, crumpled paper. He wasn't sleeping; the Leak took their sleep away after a while. Twisted fingers held the covers close to the chest.

They were always cold after this stage, no matter the temperature.

She caught herself bending forward, trying to inhale the crumpled skin. The disease beckoned as it always did, and it took all her experience and training to resist. Her fingers touched the covers, twitched as she tried not to touch the patient himself.

"Did she make it out?" the man asked. Their voice was the worst, the disharmony in it. It echoed out of a grave and forced you to come closer, to listen.

"Cybele?" she whispered. The man looked at her. "I'm not sure. I'm her friend, though. Do you know where she is?"

"I know you. I saw you watching us over the deck so many months ago, when she showed me the snowflakes."

She did not answer. His labored breath ticked the seconds off.

"She liked to visit the black church," he said. "She liked to watch the sun rise from there."

Ada waited some more, but the man only exhaled. It wore them out, talking, much as they craved it. And much as she craved an answer, the pull was becoming too much. She stood up and walked out, smoothing her jacket all the way down.

Outside, the soldier was holding on to his gun. He was fighting hard not to vomit, but for the first time in her life, Ada could not conjure any sympathy at all.

"Is he... is he...?"

"Going to be all right? What do you think?" she answered, walking past him and reaching for the stairs.

"And he was born like that?"

It caught up with her, then, compassion. She slowed down, took a breath. "It's a very rare disease, sir. You shouldn't worry— it affects less than one person in ten million. I suggest visiting Dr. Kira here, first thing in the morning. Talk about it. She will help you get it out of your mind."

Her concern shamed him back into stony silence, and they walked out.

Next morning at breakfast, the usual cliques had merged into one big, animated hydra. Ada was expecting them to be awkward with her as she walked in, cup in hand, but they had all been together for too long; after a second, they circled her, eyes gleaming.

"Have you heard?"

"I only heard the gunshots." They did not believe her; they waited for more. "All right. Anyone care to shock me with the terrible news?"

Milo stepped forward, steaming cup in hand. "Cybele is nowhere to be found. Haven't the guards come to question you yet?"

Question her — odd choice of words.

"Cybele ran off?" She could feel her heart skipping beats, but would not give them the satisfaction. "And why the fuss? She wouldn't be the first to break down in here."

"She did not break down. Or run off. She broke into the Director's office. Using very precise, very professional methods."

She looked at them startled, and they looked back, waiting.

"Did she take anything?"

"He won't tell of course," said Milo. "But she must have. They caught her down the slope, halfway to the river. I heard there was a boat waiting for her there but whoever drove it escaped when the guards grabbed her."

"Where is she now?"

"A government helicopter came for her at sunrise."

"You said government?"

The crack in her voice shut them up. Leaving her cup on the table, she walked outside and, thank their oaths, her colleagues found it in themselves to respect that and leave her alone, till the soldiers came in her room to ask her their empty questions.

"Still thinking about her?"

"You can tell?"

Six months had passed since Cybele was taken away, but Milo knew Ada well enough.

"At least the Director isn't looking at you funny anymore."

"Why would he? He's the one who hired her. And it was his decision to appoint Cybele to me in the first place. It's not like I had anything to do with her schemes."

Milo nodded and laid back. The time had not come yet for a frank discussion, and they both knew it.

Ada got up. "Going for a walk," she said. "Last days of summer."

He raised his cup, and she smiled, buttoned up her coat and walked out of the glass doors. She had been taking walks every day for the past five months, till the guards had eventually stopped tailing her and everyone had started taking her new habit for granted. Only today, instead of going towards the summit, she turned around, and went the way she had been long avoiding, the path down the slope.

The path towards the 'black church'.

It wasn't a church anymore, of course. Ages ago, it might have been the roof of one, probably considered ancient even before the Great Floods swept the old world away. The rest of the building had been submerged in mud but the top, built to withstand hail and stone, had remained, jutting out of the earth, catching the light on its dark tiles.

It took some searching but finally she noticed it, the place where the moss had been disturbed. She knelt and slid her artificial hand over it. The whole tile dislodged and a dew-covered tin caught the sunrays. There was a box there — Cybele's lunch box.

It opened easily under the pressure of her metal fingers, and Ada saw two things inside; a musty book that looked as old as the sunken church itself, and a digital data stick. She picked the tome first and slid her fingers in the old pages, trying not to inhale their rotten scent. The handwriting was hard to read, but she could tell it was some kind of ledger, a list of births and deaths in the small village that used to lie half a mile below, long before the Floods had taken it with them three millennia ago.

Only there was something wrong with the events recorded inside. First of all, it seemed that everyone who had ever been born in that village, had eventually died. Not only that, they had also died very young: at seventy, at eighty, some of them even at sixty. The most peculiar thing, though, was that the archivist had labeled all those premature deaths as 'natural causes.'

It made no sense.

"I am impressed."

The Director's voice, just a few steps behind.

A split second; her sole chance. She dropped the box and as she scrambled to pick it up, she stepped on the data stick and pushed it into the mud.

She turned around and there he was, looking at her, hands behind his back. No armed guards, she noticed. She exhaled, and looked at him; he extended his hand and she handed the book over without shutting it, trying to get a last glimpse at the handwritten litany of death.

For a moment they stood in silence, he reading, and she pushing the stick further into the ground.

"I am sorry for your friend" he said eventually, startling her. His own eyes had not widened as he looked over the ledger. "Had she told you of this?"

"No. I figured it out a few days ago," she half-lied. "Pieced some of the things she had implied together. I wanted to see if I was right."

She could see he did not believe her, and she decided to go all in.

"What does it mean, though?" she asked. "What killed this people? Why natural causes? What happened in this mountain?"

"No idea, Doctor," he smiled through his teeth. "I will study this and let you know when I understand myself."

He turned his back and left, and Ada wanted to knock him over for a moment but then she noticed his shoulders hunching and his steps growing heavy as he walked away. Kneeling to clean her boots, she picked the data stick up.

Security had tightened since Cybele's stunt, but the guard in the gate was used to Ada's artificial hand setting off the alarm; they did not notice the stick tucked inside the glove, chrome on chrome. Back to her room, she sealed the windows, took her tablet to the bathroom, sat on the edge of the bathtub and slid the stick in.

Only one folder inside, untitled. No notes, no documents, only photos: underwater graveyards, larger than anything she had ever seen, and extremely short lifespans carved on each one. Seventy years. Sixty. Forty. Some of them had pictures enshrined in them, and she could see that most of the deceased had fallen victims to the Leak before their deaths: the lined faces, the cloudy eyes, the false teeth.

This made no sense. She was no historian, and even if she were, there was precious little left from the world before the floods. However, even though the waters and the wars that followed had obliterated written records, just as they had swept away everything else, some stories had been recorded a few decades after the disaster, once the few survivors stopped fighting and scraping for food, settled down and started to rebuild over the ruins. They spoke of famine, and salted earth and the fires that broke out in the abandoned cities, consuming what was left. They spoke of the Himalayan ice melting, flooding the world a second time, prolonging their struggle. They spoke of the diseases they had to combat without access to hospitals or medicine, the wounds that took decades to heal, their cancers that had to wait a hundred years for previously known cures to be re-invented. Yet there was no mention of a Leaking epidemic in their scarce tellings, no word of people simply wasting away with time till they were dead.

A knock on her room's door. Oh well. It had taken him long enough.

She got up, opened the bathroom door, crossed the sitting room. The Director was on the outside. Again, no armed guards with him. He inclined his head, and she stepped back to let him in. The door closed behind him.

"So, you really did not know," he pointed out. "I apologize for the bluff. I had to make sure you were not allied with them."

"Them?"

"The Pures. Cybele's little terrorist group." She kept staring at him, and he sighed. "Can I have the data stick, or whatever it was? You would not have given me the book so easily, if you weren't holding on to something else."

"Of course. Can I have an explanation in return? I've been working on the Leak for the last two hundred and seventy-five years. Milo was here a century before me. This," she pointed at the tablet, still sitting on the bathroom sink, "looks like something we should've known."

"I know. I apologize, Doctor; I did not enjoy keeping secrets myself, but the position of the Director came with caveats."

"Yet you let me find it. You could've stopped me before I reached the church."

"Again, I do not enjoy keeping secrets, even as I understand the need for them. They are the death of science. "He leaned on her wall, arms crossed. "Speaking of secrets, by now you might have realized how your protégé had us all fooled. I invited her over after encountering her impressive research on prosthetics and regenerative techniques. And at first, she seemed the most dedicated of all of us. Yet it seems, she never meant to heal the Leak."

"Oh? Then what was she doing up here? The view isn't that magnificent."

He did not crack a smile. "I believe she meant to sneak one of the patients out, or at least secure samples and photos, and spread them into the general population." He paused for a moment, glancing at her, then went on. "You see, the Pures believe the disease and its conclusion, death, to be our natural state — something to strive for, instead of a horrible illness. Which is why Cybele wormed her way up here, so she could find a way to spread the word and, maybe, the disease itself." He scrutinized her face for a moment. "This is the first you are hearing of that."

"It is." Cybele as she knew her was shredded; she would pick the pieces later, rebuild a new Cybele. Out of the maelstrom though, one thing remained. "She did make you wonder, didn't she? You did ponder, could she possibly be right?"

He smiled a tight smile. "Perhaps? Doesn't the sight of the Leak strike a chord a bit too deep for comfort? What other disease does that to us, after so long?" He stopped leaning on the wall, and took a step towards her, hands in his pockets. "Most governments try to keep it under wraps, but the archaeologists do find unsettling bits from time to time, things like the ledger and the graveyards. There are old texts, stories that would only make sense if we were mortal once."

"You mean, if we all eventually contracted the Leak and simply died?"

"Exactly. With our antediluvian history lost, anyone can theorize, can't they? And this is why you and I are paid to stay holed up here: someone always digs something up and starts wondering — and eventually, they become enthralled with this idea of death as the true natural order. Some of them even find our little Institute and crawl to us, like Cybele did. For these people, the Leak is the ultimate confirmation of their theories." He paused for the briefest second. "I admire their perseverance, yet in the end I am a healer, just like you are. No matter what I think of their theories, I do not have the patience to entertain their madness."

"What if they're right? What if this is the way we are meant to end? What if we were short-lived, once, so very long before the Floods that we had lost even the memory of it when the waters came?"

"Care to tell that to the people withering in the basement? That it is all right to suffer as they do, that they are doing their ancestors proud?"

No. The answer came unbidden and she silenced it, but it hung between them for a whole ripe moment before dissipating.

She held back for a second, then another. Finally, she sighed.

"What will happen to her?"

"It is never my decision. All I could do was tell the agents who came to question me that the Leak drives some of us mad and they should take pity on her, see her as another casualty of this disease. I doubt I made any difference, though. The last thing the government wants is more cultists."

"Why hide this truth from us researchers, though? Why not tell us, a few decades in?" And then, "Why not tell everyone in the world about this mortality theory? We are still a democracy, are we not?"

He was silent for a few seconds, and something of this silence crept into her bones.

"Because once the idea gets into someone's head that the Leak is the way things should be, Doctor, ugly things start to happen to the believers. The pull becomes stronger. More visceral. It tugs at people at a whole other level. And for those of us who have looked at a patient's eyes, the sensation becomes irresistible. Do you understand what I am saying?"

She could read between the lines well enough. "We get sick too."

He gave no reply, yet she found the answer in his eyes, and it chilled her.

She did not want the Leak. She did not want to get sick and then waste away. How could she? How could anyone? How could anyone believe, that this horror was the natural order of things? Cybele had been mad to think so. This was a disease, and like every disease it had to have a cure.

"What should I do?"

"Work." His smile startled her. It was not a pretty sight, like light coming down on old ruins. "Work harder than before, to find the cure and prove your friend and the Pures, or any other cultist, wrong.

Because if we don't find a cure, Doctor, if there isn't one, then they might be right and the moment you believe that will be a painful one."

No, this could not happen. She had things to do, they all had. A bucket list. Fishing. She looked at him and then nodded, chrome fingers limp at her side.

"Good night, Doctor. I trust you will keep this entirely to yourself. Better not to place any more people in danger, don't you think so?"

"Of course."

She escorted him out, and closed the door.

She would not tell, he was right about that. No reason to drag Milo and the rest into that. No reason to put them in such danger. She would sleep on it, then wake up and start working, really working. Now that she knew, she would request permission again to dig among the Institute's roots. This time, he would not have reason to deny her. She would find out why the Leak called to all of them, the real reason, not Cybele's delusions. After all, what else was left to do?

A chord a bit too deep, the Director had said. She went to pick the tablet, stare at the graves again, but stopped in her tracks.

Tomorrow would come and with it, questions. But tonight, the sky was clear and the Institute was silent. The world's buried truths could wait for one last, peaceful night.

About the story

For a story that deals with death, hope and our human lust for achieving ever more, "Any Old Disease" has decidedly pulp origins. I have never seen 2012, the disaster movie directed by Roland Emmerich, but one image in the trailer stuck to mind: a Tibetan monk, looking up to see a tidal wave dwarfing the Himalaya. A few years later we began playing Ivory Towers, a role-playing game where after a flood, the world has been beautifully rebuilt – by corporations. I played as a soldier who becomes increasingly curious about the lost world that came before him, the world he thinks he knew about.

Thinking of the past as a well-documented time with just a few mysteries sprinkled in-between to keep things spicy, is a common mistake. David Macaulay's *Motel of the Mysteries* illustrates that best: in 4022 a motel is excavated and future archaeologists are excited, interpreting every single thing they find, from a toothbrush to a bathplug, as an important artifact. The picture of the lead archaeologist with a toilet seat on his head, purposely resembling Sophia Schliemann bedecked in Troy's gold, is meant to be humorous but to me, it was a revelation: we can never know what came before and everything we think we know, is covered in our own assumptions. My love of history had suddenly turned from a diligent pursuit of knowledge to a romantic quest.

Not that that I consider this a bad thing.

With these ideas in mind, I began to write a horror story about a mysterious disease, a sinister Director and the stalwart doctor who sets out to discover the truth. Soon though, it mutated into something else.

It might have been the face of my Godfather, a surgeon who has not rested a day since he began work and won't rest as long as someone needs him. Maybe it was the article I wrote on the pursuit of immortality from China's courts to the USSR and up to the transhumanist movement. Or my growing fear of an environmental catastrophe, sweeping us away.

It might also have been that, amidst a deluge of bad news from all over the world, humans keeps insisting on a better future – no matter how badly we mess up our eternal pursuit. After all, I was taught at school that our Greek word for human –anthropos– literally means *looking upwards*.

Of course, as I was writing, none of this entered my mind. I was just following Dr Ada as she unraveled the secrets of her Institute one by one, as familiar faces changed into something unknown and signs of wrongness kept unsettling her, nudging her to find the truth. In a way, it is a gothic tale, a heroine trapped in a mountaintop estate racing to discover its long buried secret before they drive her to an awful fate. While my plot pays homage to its pulp roots, other elements had crept in and made the story mine — as is always the case when you write. And every time someone asks a question about the worldbuilding or the characters, I uncover a new inspiration which I had not even considered in the course of writing.

I can only be grateful so many others have liked it in the meantime.

A question for the author

Q: Are you a Luddite? Or do you have the latest and greatest technology?

A: Not a Luddite at all; I love technology, and recognize it as a major factor in many positive social changes I am now benefiting from. Having said that, I need to step away from my screens more often, before I fuse with them.

About the author

Dimitra Nikolaidou is a PhD candidate, researching role-playing games and speculative fiction at the Aristotle University of Thessaloniki in Thessaloniki,

Greece. She is the chief editor and in-house writer for Archetypo Publications. Finally, she teaches creative writing focused on speculative fiction at *Tales of the Wyrd*. She is always planning trips in Europe and excursions in the woods, and sometimes even manages to take them.

@D_Nikolaidou

Velaya, the Dreaming City

Six parts after Dunsany

Beston Barnett

Part 1

I set out for Velaya as a young man, having only just pledged to wed. I was to marry Belqis, flower of our village and light of my eyes, in whose father's orchards I had played since my childhood. Our marriage should have been enough for a lifetime of happiness. But I believed then—as so many young fools do—that dreams were the currency of happiness, and I carried with me dreams as yet unredeemed. And though I tried to conceal it, Belqis, my betrothed, sensed my dissatisfaction and, knowing its source, spoke to me, saying:

"Always you have shared with me your dreams of Velaya. You have whispered to me of silver domes and white carved stone, of miraculous waters which run in aqueducts through strolling parks, of red and gold kites which fly from the cliffs and gild the sky, and of so many other wonders that for me the Dreaming City lives in the sound of your voice. Always it has been your dream to visit far-off Velaya and know its mysteries.

"And yet, once we are married, it is possible that duties to our fields and orchards and to family and to our as yet unborn children—think of our beautiful children, my love!—may keep you from ever travelling to such dreamed-of distant lands. I am selfish and do not wish to bear that disappointment. Therefore, though each day apart will be a trial, I say: go now to Velaya and return to me with eyes brim full of silver and green and red and gold, eyes that have beheld the Dreaming City. For though I love you now and with all I know of my heart, it may be that I will love the man who returns to me from Velaya even more."

Thus—as ever—did Belqis amaze me with her generosity.

Of course, I protested.

I said, "The duties you speak of are to me nothing but joys."

And also, "Our full and happy lives could admit of no regrets."

And also, "My dreams of Velaya are a child's dreams, but my dreams of the coming together of our lives are the dreams of the man I wish to become."

But Belqis knew my heart, and she overcame my protestations. And truthfully —young and foolish though I was—I knew myself blessed even then to be understood so well and trusted so completely.

And so Velaya rose up triumphant in my mind's eye.

I set out by cart and was soon come to lands beyond any I had known. I traveled by overgrown tracks through fields cultivated with grain and by wide highways that the legionnaires had of old hewn through the impassable forests between cities. Coming over rocky wastes and through orchards of olives, I had my first sight of the sea and felt myself remade in its grandeur and its sadness.

And though I was clumsy with the language of the dock-hands in that first port, I was able by signs and nodding to book passage over the sea and to come finally to the yellow shores of that great desert land of which Velaya is the very jewel and heart and center. From there, caravans of camels in long trains came and went daily. Here were found traders, journeymen, diplomats, shepherds, but also pilgrims, and these were my true kin —the pilgrims—those that had been granted visions of Velaya in dreams.

When I had replenished my stores and purchased a blanket and hired a camel-puller, I too joined a caravan and left at dawn for the last four days of my pilgrimage.

That first night in the desert was cold; a cold of open spaces like none I had known. As the drivers settled their camels into corrals, I huddled with three pilgrims around the remnants of our cooking fire, and we drank the clear local liquor called *raktash* and each of us was fired by the *raktash* with bright longing for Velaya.

And out of this bright longing, the woman who had traveled from distant lands far to the West spoke, saying:

Part 2

"It is said of the gods of Velaya that they are fierce but also generous, that their dreams dwell often along the white and shining cliffs, and that in their dreams, miracles are worked. For it is within the power of their miraculous dreams to grant the gift of *flight*.

"Aspirants travel great distances to petition this gift of the gods. Settling in the squatter's quarter known as the Aerie, aspirants build themselves the nests of sticks and mud which will be their homes for at least the next season and often much longer. During the days they lie in their uncovered nests, absorbing the rays of the sun, taking the lightness of the sun into them, willing themselves to lighten. Then in the cool spring evenings, they descend in their white robes to the taverns and meeting places of the city, and there recite the light-filled 'cloud poems' for which Velaya is justly renowned.

"As the sun fills their bodies with lightness, so aspirants fill with a floating feeling, and in the summer they are often seen wearing lead weights around arms and ankles as ballast. Much of their poetry in this season eulogizes the peculiar sensation of untying the weights from their limbs in the evening, of experiencing that weightlessness which presages the hoped-for gift. In this season too they begin work on the red and gold paper constructions which they will fly from the lower cliffs with such drama during the kite festival.

"It is in the autumn that aspirants often decide to petition the gods. It is not a decision shared or discussed, but must be reached alone, known by the lightness in the heart, by the tense spreading of invisible wings. Many, through doubt or humility, never decide. But on a clear morning in the first cool days after summer, a small white-robed figure may be seen climbing alone the Dawn Stair and mounting to the heights of Veliara, tallest of the white cliffs, though it does not face Velaya as the others do, but is hidden and turned away behind a great knee of limestone rubble.

"And what happens then numbers among the great mysteries of Velaya. For it is not known if there is some right phrasing or secret password or if perhaps the heart of the aspirant is weighed against that of a feather or if it is purity or yearning or some inborn talent or simply the dream of gods whose dreams must of necessity be ineffable. The aspirant makes his petition and steps from the cliff. The gods dream and judge. And some aspirants—most, it is said—end there at the base of Veliara, and their bleached bones remain uncounted, for the base of the cliff of Veliara is sacred ground and to visit there is forbidden.

"But there are some—a few? one a year? a decade? a generation?—who are caught in the cupped hands of the gods' dreaming and who fly."

The woman from the distant West paused then and drank. We all drank, each in turn—the *raktash* like hot sand that singes the throat and afterwards consoles it—before she continued.

"And there are those who say that long since passed are the days in which the gods of Velaya heard petitions. The city fills with white-robed aspirants, yet fewer and fewer climb the Dawn Stair each year. *Where are these chosen flyers,* they say, *aloft on god-dreams?* And in the dark corners of taverns there are others who whisper that the gods' interest is only with the pile of aspirant bones at the base of

Veliara and not with those that would fly above it.

"But as for me, I am unwavering. From my youngest days have I dreamed of flying and known those dreams to be the best part of myself and true.

"And one day I will take my place among the flyers above Velaya."

We stared into what embers of the fire remained then, each of us inhabiting the image of the city that our minds conjured glowing there in the coals, and I sensed the others drift one by one into sleep.

But I lay awake, I know not how long after, with my mind in the jaws of frightful premonitions. A veil seemed pulled aside, and all was revealed and inverted and churning. *The city is a trap,* I thought, and my thoughts were like jaws that closed and closed again. I saw a procession of young men and women with broken wings, sun-blind, their limbs contorted. *The city is a trap. It calls to the gullible, to the pilgrims, to the dreamers like myself, and it eats their dreams.*

I saw the pile of bones at the base of Veliara, felt myself pressed beneath them.

I slept.

In the morning was a great hubbub of packers and camel-pullers and coffee wallahs calling across the expanse of cold, spent fires. I stood, wrapped in my blanket. In the noise and the smell of the coffee and the gray light of the new day, my last night's imaginings paled. I thought of Velaya and Belqis, the dreamed-of city and my beautiful wife. Both awaited me, and by this I knew myself a pilgrim twice blessed, who followed two stars. Gathering my few belongings, I thought, *And what if the allure of Velaya eclipses that of Belqis? What if its red and gold kites, its white walls, its taverns full of poetry, what if these seduce me and make me forget my heart?* Yet—after one month, after two—I would return to my Belqis and tell her what I had felt and seen, for the tale of such beauty must have an audience, and always Belqis had been that audience for me. I believed that I knew myself; that I would return to her. For though Velaya filled my mind with imagined colors, Belqis still filled my heart.

Velaya might be a trap for some, but not for me.

All that sweltering day I sat and swayed on the princely hump of my camel as the great caravan spread out around me and advanced. And at end of day, we came again to a camp in the desert where the day's caravan heading northward from Velaya met our southward-heading caravan, and again there was the chaos of stocks and tents and animals and cooking fires scattered like a wide mirror of the stars which are themselves scattered in a band across the night sky. And again that evening my three companions and I reclined together around our small fire and ate and passed the local liquor *raktash* that so opens the hearts of travellers, one to another.

Then into that tranquility that descends upon the desert at day's end, the young man from the distant North spoke, saying:

Part 3

"I have heard it said of the gods of Velaya that they are loving but shy. That they love their people is certain, evidenced by the many miracles they have wrought in their city, chiefest among these the Miracle of the Waters, which rise up in the desert city in green pools and playful fountains to delight and succor its people. Yet the gods of Velaya are also shy, timid of applicants, unwilling to reveal themselves except to the most pure and the most devout. But in their love, they have left stones hidden in and below the city which the pure and devout may find and with which they may commune with the gods. For it is thus that the gods find the miracles they bestow upon Velaya: by mining in the hearts of men.

"There was a man stranded at the base of a cliff deep in the desert, lost, dying of thirst; this was the first applicant. How he came to be there, how he came by such purity of heart and devotion of spirit, these things are not known. But there in his distress he found a stone, and this was the first of the Dreaming Stones. It was a sand-smoothed oblong of jade, and through it, clasping it to him, the man communed with a god; this was the first of the gods of Velaya, who is called simply Vel, and who mined in the heart of the man through the Dreaming Stone and found there Velaya's first miracle: the Miracle of the Waters.

"He was the first applicant; since then, there have been many. Successive generations of applicants have come and striven and searched and some—the pure, the devout—have found the stone they sought, and the miracles they carried in their hearts have transformed Velaya into the jewel of the desert. The massive statues of the First Dreamers, the tiered Night Gardens, the filigreed temple of Vel-Abir—all these were miracles wrought by stone-finders of old. The Dawn Stair itself was among the earliest miracles: the heart-wish of a father whose daughter loved above all else the flying of kites; his plain river stone appeared to him one evening at the bottom of a humble pot of soup.

"Many applicants are miners or prospectors or vendors in the gemstone markets for which Velaya is renowned, where they daily handle seraphinite, jade, epidote, chrysoprase, beryl. Others work in infrastructure, shoring up stone work, re-routing water systems, sculpting architectural ornament, or simply cleaning the floors of palaces and homes. Always and at every hour, applicants search for their Dreaming Stone, listening for its distinct call, opening their hearts in purity and devotion. An applicant serves the city and his dearest wish is to have the next great miracle—the cliff statues, the gardens, the stairs—called forth from his heart through the stone of his dreams, and thus to live on forever as a part of the city itself.

"And, yes, there are those who say that many years have come and gone since Velaya was re-fashioned by miracle-stones. They say that the city is too big now, too impure with commerce, or that the last Dreaming Stone has long since been found. Or in darker moods, some mutter that perhaps the gods find their nourishment no longer with the pure and their stones, but with the suffering of the applicant who goes blind cutting gemstones or who is crushed in the mines beneath the city or who is worked to death cleaning, every day, year upon year, the palaces, the walls, the sewers."

The young man paused, and drank as if to rid his mouth of a disagreeable taste.

"But as for me, I am undeterred. Since earliest memory have I dreamed of holding a green stone to my breast, holding it and calling forth wonders. And I believe that one day, when I have hallowed the city in my eye and in my heart—with purity, with devotion, with humility—then shall I find my place among the miracle-workers of Velaya.

"For this was I made."

We lay then silent around the dying fire, each of us awed and entranced by the Northern man's story. The Dreaming City shone before my mind's eye—as I knew it must before the others'—wonderful, exotic, like a child's glass marble given by a parent returning from long travels, alight with possibility.

And yet, as the others drifted into sleep, the image of the city tilted in my mind. I saw it as from below, up from the blackness of the mines that coil through its foundations, and there I saw old men and women, frail and blind, who struggled through those tunnels ceaselessly and in vain. And I saw that those tunnels were the entrails of the city, its very intestines, and all those zealous seekers no more than digesting meat trapped in a horrible peristalsis. *The city is a trap,* I repeated to myself.

The words echoed, the coils tightened. *The city is a trap.*

Somehow I slept.

The next morning broke with the same confusion of activity as before, and yet I felt it overlain with a new sense of urgency and reverence. The Dreaming City waited only two days ride to the South. We pilgrims rode lost in thought as brides to a distant wedding who in their thoughts take leave of their former lives and prepare as best they can to be transformed. And all that sun-bleached day I meditated on what it might mean to be disappointed by Velaya. What if I found its streets dirty, its vistas uninspiring, its palaces gaudy, its gardens wasted, its denizens petty, its meeting places unwelcoming, its waters untended and unclean, and all my many dreams, mirages? What if I found more truth in the eyes of its beggars, than in the hauteur of its gods? These thoughts were terrible. I would be broken. And would I then return to Belqis and ask her to fulfil her vows to a broken man?

And thinking thus I remembered Belqis, my other pilgrim's star. I remembered her not as simply an audience or a symbol of home, but as she truly was—generous and understanding and kind. I knew that she would accept and remake me, that I might be dispirited for a time but that I would be remade in our lives together and in the lives of our children, and that one day we might all smile together at the dreams of my earnest youth. A weight lifted from me, like a fever breaking. I believed I knew myself. I believed I knew Belqis. And as we arrived at the final camp and the porters flew about their accustomed tasks, I thought, *I shall see what there is to be seen of Velaya, whatever that may be, and I shall return to my beloved and tell of it.*

The city might be a trap for some, but not for the man for whom Belqis waits.

And as the preparations for the night's camp began, there were pilgrims who said they could see already the white cliffs of Velaya off to the South, but I could make out only what seemed a sand storm, a shimmering white smudge on the horizon.

Just as in earlier nights, my companions and I built a small fire, spread blankets, and shared out dried apricots and patties of lentils. We passed the local liquor *raktash* in a small gourd between us, hand-to-hand and solemnly: a libation. It would be our last night as a company, and our hearts were so full with the awesome nearness of the Dreaming City that I expected no one to break the thoughtful trance which had come upon us with the cold and the dark. Thus were we all surprised when the silent woman— a woman from far to the East by her clothes, whom I, for one, had assumed spoke none of our common tongues—

began to tell of her dreams in a clear and quiet voice, saying:

Part 4

"Among my people we have an idiom: *wary as the gods of Velaya.* We say this of the baker who will not share his recipe with his apprentice, or of the midwife who will teach no one the secrets of her trade. That the gods of Velaya keep secrets is known. Of the secrets of flight and of communion we have had eulogies already; but they keep also secrets for changing lead to gold, and making broken things whole, and living eternally young. And why are these secrets kept so dear? Are the gods given to spite or jealousy? Or might they perhaps be wise to allow only the few and the dedicated to learn the working of such miracles as might undo less worthy supplicants?

"The madrasas of the Dreaming City are built on this simple faith: that both wary *and* wise are the gods of Velaya.

"Students flock to the madrasas from all the lands that we know, and from the moment they step through the East Gate, their lives are bounded by ceremony and study. During their first years, most complement their research by taking apprenticeship with the glassblowers or the metalsmiths or in the guild of the nurses. After graduation, many may take up the mantle of professorship or medical practice, but the final stage in the lives of the scholars of Velaya is always solitary and secret study, for it is in mimicking the gods themselves—*wary and wise*—that they hope to discern that which their dreams have intimated: the recipes, formulas, incantations, codes, and mechanisms of the miraculous.

"Of the great madrasas, two dominate: the alchemists' university and the hospital. At the lower levels, these institutions operate as schools, as wards, as laboratories and libraries; they buzz with students, patients, and journeymen, all moving about their labors. But as scholars attain the higher levels, treading spiral stairs into the towers that sprout from these centers of learning like shoots in spring seeking upward for a purer air, so their silence deepens. In the highest rooms—within the very domes which so distinguish the city—the most learnéd study in deep solitude where the only sound is the turning of pages and the scritching of pen against parchment. And even above that, it is said, there are floating rooms hidden by art of magic in the upper air where adepts neither read, nor write, nor discourse at all, but simply stare into the secret mysteries of the universe.

"Of course, such institutions must have their detractors: students embittered by failed examinations or families dissatisfied with the care given a loved one. The scholars of Velaya, they say, neglect the world around them for the sky above and lose their way in mazes of their own making. In seeking the miraculous, the scholars wish to be gods themselves and so must fail.

"And perhaps, whisper the spiteful to one another, the whole towering hierarchy of study and sacrifice is as a honeypot laid by the gods—oh so wise and wary, the gods—who would lay a honeypot to feed off the best and brightest, their would-be usurpers.

"But as for me, I am undaunted."

Here, the Eastern woman paused and raised the gourd of *raktash* to each of us in turn, looking steadily into each pair of eyes from beneath the folds of her hood before continuing.

"In my dreams, I stand below the silver domes with a balm in my hand, a miraculous balm to heal the sick and make whole the maimed. And in that dream, the sick and the maimed come to me, and I heal them and, by my hand, I make them whole.

"Be it prophecy or be it illusion, I shall follow whither such a dream leads, because it is a good dream, and because it is mine."

Silence settled on us then, and we lay staring into the last lit embers of our fire. The Eastern woman's tale had been so eloquent, her dream so noble, we each of us felt that a grace had been laid upon our little camp and a blessing upon our dreams. I felt certain that the premonitions which had haunted me on previous nights would not recur.

But as the others closed their eyes and the dim fire gave way entirely to the dimmer light of cold desert stars, I began to think of Velaya in the abstract. Of what does it dream?—Velaya—for it is called the Dreaming City, and not the City of Dreams. Are the dreams of the city and of its gods one? And what if the city's dreams are of men that never leave, but circle endlessly its siren streets, seeking but never finding dreams of their own?

Then, of a sudden, the image of Velaya —that image which had been in my mind since my earliest memories and which had grown in these final days of my pilgrimage to fill every corner of my inner sky—that image tilted again. Now I saw it not from belowground, where its mines twisted and turned, but from above, where countless layered labyrinths made of naught but wind and vapor ornamented the air between the domes and radiated outward and upward in towers and coronae. And through these labyrinths, hidden in the air, crawled old men and women, scholars, always alone, always seeking but never finding, their robes too threadbare to keep out the cold. And I saw that if the mines were the digestive tracts of Velaya, then these insubstantial mazes above the city were its brain matter, and the scholars lost there were as its very neurons. And I saw that this beast of a city nourished itself on a steady stream of pilgrims but shat out only bones. And I saw that the great breathing of this parasitic beast, squatting there one day's ride through the desert, was the nightly going out and gathering in of its dreams,

dreams like lures, like siren song, like golden netting, and these dream-lures were made in the crucible of its inhabitants' desperation and longing, made under great pressure and flung out in invisible waves from its trembling need.

The city is a trap, I thought, *but not for me. I am neither flyer nor miner nor scholar, and I have Belqis.* I would pass through unharmed, like a white egret that flies over the swamp and returns, unsullied.

My mind calmed. I shifted beneath my blanket and turned on my side and thought that now I would finally rest. A pleasant silence of sleepers and cold stars spread out around me. Tomorrow, all the colors of Velaya awaited.

And with that I came fully awake. Another scenario visited me—a possibility I had not before considered—and it set me shivering, for it had the halo of truth about it. What if Velaya seemed at first a disappointment and, after a week of seeing its uninspired sights, I was ready to depart and prepare what disappointing words I would say to Belqis, but then I spied there something colorful and vibrant, something truly *of* the city of my many dreams? Of course, I would have to stay and explore it—a café where poets gathered or a crumbling temple in the gardens, a place where something unfolded which was worthy of being described to my Belqis. And after I had learned enough of the vain poets or the maudlin temple and was preparing to leave once again, what if I should stumble across some other image or experience which seemed to speak more to the heart of the mystery of the Velaya for which I had first set out? A little girl building a kite with her grandfather perhaps, or a green-robed monk planting a yellow flower, or the great cliffs glowing from a certain perspective in a certain light. Would I not then stay and explore a while longer, if only so that my tales for Belqis would be that much more captivating?

And with each new delay, my absence from Belqis would grow. The longer I was away, the more amazing my stories would have to be on my return. Otherwise, how could I explain to her why I had stayed away so long? I imagined myself desperate —after six months, after a year, after five years—struggling to find something, always just around the corner in Velaya, worthy of telling my Belqis. Something amazing enough to heal the wound of our long separation. After five years, what could possibly be amazing enough? A miraculous balm? A god-stone? A pair of god-gifted wings?

Now was I frozen in fear, feverish, trapped in the coils of my own premonitions. I saw the pile of bones, the mines like intestines, the mazes pulsing in the air, and I saw myself following a trail of glittering clues through the streets, pacing out mandalas, the true Velaya always just ahead, and I, desperate and in despair. And what then would become of my Belqis?

No. Sometime well before dawn, I made a decision. I would not say goodbye. I would not face the disbelief and disappointment of my companions.

I arose and padded through the camp and found my indignant camel-puller and informed him of my change of plans.

I would not venture on to Velaya.

Part 5

And that is the story of my life. The central story, the story on which the rest teeters. A coward's less-than-heroic story about a long journey and an abandoned dream. That is how I viewed it for many years: an abandoned dream.

I returned to my village and married Belqis. At first I lied to everyone: I told fanciful but brief tales of the wonders I had seen. To those who asked why I hadn't stayed longer, I said that the time away from my beloved had been too painful, that I had been eager to start our lives together. This was half true, and Belqis, caught up in the excitement of the wedding, allowed me these half-truths for a time.

But my wife is an observant woman. After we had been living together for some months, she began very delicately to probe my stories, and I broke down almost at once. In real torment of soul, I told how three nights of terrible premonitions in the desert had defeated a lifetime of dreams. I recall how we sat at our little table long after the village slept, drinking the tart early cider our orchards produce in that season and speaking in low tones by the light of a single candle. And how she did not reproach me but looked at me all through our conversation with tender compassion. Yet still I felt myself a failure.

"I failed the first and simplest test of Velaya, a test of the resilience of my dreams. I am revealed a coward."

"My beloved, you were made to choose between the city and me. It is not cowardly to choose love. I honor you."

"And I honor you and love you … yet I cannot help but feel unworthy now of that love."

And Belqis held my hand and, from that night, she seemed to love me as much as ever she had or even more.

And in the years that followed, our fields were fruitful and our flock thrived and our village prospered. We were blessed with three children, two girls and a boy, all beautiful and full of life. In motherhood, Belqis grew in beauty and wisdom. We were blessed. And yet at times—in truth, *often*—I seemed to see our blessings as through a veil, a veil that separated me from my feelings and from other people. A veil that filtered color from the world. At these times, I felt myself a hollow husband, a hollow father.

Rarely in those years did we mention my journey, and never once did Belqis reproach me for my failures. Never, at least, until the naming of our tavern.

For some time, she had talked of opening a tavern such as our village lacked, a proper place for travelers to eat and pass the evening, and for village meetings and dances in the colder months. I supported her, and when the structure was complete and the first fire was lit in the barroom hearth, Belqis showed me the signboard that would hang above the front door. The board was carved and colored wood, white cliffs against a blue sky, with the words, *The Dreaming City,* engraved across them in painted silver.

It had been so long since those once magical words had passed my lips; I felt stung, mocked. I hesitated, then spoke carefully.

"I did not know you had decided on a name."

Belqis did not look at me, but smiled at the floor. "It is a beautiful name for a tavern," she said. "Travelers will recognize it, and the village will find it exotic and exciting... Do you like it?"

I sensed that she was tense, that maybe the whole project for this tavern had been leading to this moment, to this sign and this name—that now was the time to show my gratitude for her years of forbearance—but I didn't trust myself to speak. Coward that I am, I made an ambivalent "mmm" sound and nodded.

The tavern was a success. Belqis took some pride in preparing the days' meals and the nights' rooms, in welcoming travelers and introducing them to our local cider. She seemed in her element there, a fish in good water. I spent more time in the fields or teaching the children to tend the flock and the garden and the orchards. Of course, I visited the barroom some nights, though I was uncomfortable with the travelers and their talk.

But one cool autumn evening with the fire's warm glow burnishing the few faces in the room, a young man traveling alone began to talk of Velaya, and it was as if his voice spoke to me across space and time, from another fire in the desert far away and years ago, but immediate, present. He said he loved birds and had dreamed as a child that he could speak to them. Later, he had heard that the secret to the language of birds could be found in a distant city far to the South. Many had scoffed, insisting that the birds had no language or that the stories of men who spoke with birds were only legends, but he remained true to his dreams.

I was transfixed.

When he had finished, Belqis looked at me and away—subtly and quick—and then she offered a glass of cider to the young man who loved birds.

To the room, she said, "A glass of cider and a bowl of stew on the house for any traveler who tells a story of the Dreaming City!"

There were no more storytellers that night, but word spread, and eventually our tavern became known throughout the countryside and beyond as a trading post for the lore of Velaya. Pilgrims would travel many miles off their routes to spend an evening or two at *The Dreaming City* and to share a story. We heard from warriors who dreamed of invincible swords, and lovers who dreamed of fairy brides, and would-be wizards who dreamed of taming fiery dragons. And sometimes—as the months became years —if the night was slow or the weather was bad, I might volunteer a story of my own journey. Never of the city itself, but of the dock-hands I had encountered and the sailing ship, or of the sounds and smells of the great caravans.

And am I now content? Am I healed? I am still ashamed of my brush with the city. And yet also I am haunted by a kind of wary nostalgia for the road and its mysteries. I am not entirely content, but neither am I the hollow man I was for a time. There is color again.

And tonight after a late evening of stories in the tavern, as I helped Belqis into bed and lay down beside her—wise Belqis, clever Belqis, flower of our village and light of my eyes—she turned to me and spoke to me softly.

She said, "Our flocks and our orchards do well. The tavern prospers."

"Yes, my love," I said and touched her gray hair.

She said, "Our children are grown and married and have children of their own. You have taught them to tend the farm and I have taught them to tend the tavern, and our children and our grandchildren do these things well and with love."

"Yes, my love," I said and touched her shoulder.

She said, "All these things we have done with love and now we have time."

"Yes, my love," I said and took her hand, though I did not yet know what she meant.

And she said, "We can go to Velaya together."

Part 6

I am Belqis and the dream of Belqis and I am old.

I was old already when we set out. Old and dying, if truth be known, though it had been my constant concern in those last few months to hide my growing infirmity from my husband and my children.

They were not so very difficult to deceive. My children worried about their own children, not about me, and this relieved and comforted me, for it is as things should be between the generations. As for my husband, I believe he saw me still as a young maid—the dream of Belqis he had returned to all those years ago— and I loved him for this harmless delusion and indulged him.

But I could not deceive myself. What had at first seemed the common ache and stiffness of age revealed itself over the course of some months to be a creeping paralysis. I could no longer turn my hips or unbend my back to reach the shelves in the pantry, my ankles would not flex, and my right hand was perfectly wooden, like the false claw of an amputee, so that I poured cider now only with my left. I was become an old fire-ravaged tree. I succumbed branch by branch, the sap hardened, the xylem and cambium no longer coursed with living water: I knew that soon I would be only pith, only dead wood.

And so I determined that we should travel as aged pilgrims to Velaya, to the Dreaming City, where my husband could at last complete the great interrupted arc of his life, and I, like a canny cat that when its time has come slinks away from family and friends, I could go there to die.

We left with fanfare and the blessings of the whole village, and I, swaddled in quilts, waved from our hired carriage and smiled and wept and knew that I was dying and never to see my children again. And that was hard—very hard—but I have always endeavored to live gracefully, and I chose to die gracefully as well.

After only two days, we had traveled farther than I had ever traveled before. After two weeks, nothing at all was recognizable to me: not the language men spoke, not the trees, not the very color of the earth. In the mornings, birds I did not know sang songs I had never before heard. My body continued to stiffen, but through the apertures of my ears and eyes, a new lightness entered me, made of awe and surprise and a comforting sense of our smallness when considered against the expanse of the wide world.

And still I did not speak to my husband of dying. Not until at last I beheld the sea—the true, storied sea, wide, steel gray, implacable, against which all human conceit is but loose sand—only then did my unwillingness to speak of dying fall away from me at last. We booked passage, and there on deck, amid the strange back-and-forth calls of the sailors as they clambered through the rigging and the sharp smell of sea wrack, I pressed my husband's hand.

"Now that we have left the road for the sea and can no more turn back, we must speak of difficult things."

"My love?"

"You know that my body is failing, that I walk only with great difficulty, that my hands have stiffened to such a degree that I can no longer feed myself. You take my arm and you guide me, you put the spoon in my mouth, and you do these things lovingly. I am made to feel young and loved and I am grateful. But we must speak the truth of these things." I held his eyes. "My husband, I am dying."

"Of course you are not... Or we are dying together, yes, and will do so for many happy years. My love, let us not talk of such things, but enjoy the sea breeze and the sun. Here, I will adjust your chair to better catch the light."

I said, "I have a disease. A paralysis is moving through my body, slowly, stilling my hands, my legs, my back. It will reach my lungs or my heart soon. Sooner than you have imagined... I am sorry."

He looked at me, amazed, but I would not look away, though tears started from my eyes.   "Then we will turn back," he said. "If it is as you say, I will speak to the captain immediately and we will turn back. I must bear the blame for encouraging this pilgrimage. We will go home where you can rest and you can mend."

And my husband made as if to stand and go, but I spoke softly, so that he bent to hear me.

"I will not mend and there is not time. I am sorry. It has been a good life with you and our families and our children and the orchards and the tavern—a life full of love—but it is ending. And now I wish to see Velaya."

Then he sank before me and held my knees and wept.

We said much more to one another, that day and in the days that followed, but we did not turn around, and gradually my husband came to support my resolve. And though my condition worsened, so that I was more like a bent plank of wood than a woman when finally we made port, he bathed me and cared for me and passed the evenings of our sea voyage with descriptions of the great caravans he had known of old.

But the port town, when we alighted, seemed diminished from the bustling center he had described, and the wide caravanserai with its many stables and markets was pitifully empty. I saw disappointment on my husband's face and also confusion, and I, in my debility, could do little to help. Eventually we found someone in the dusty market who would take us the four days to Velaya on camelback, though our guide's fare was exorbitant and his camel seemed skinny and old, even to one who had never seen a camel before.

We set out the next day, and the going was hard for me. We rode together on the one camel, my husband and I, because I was so light and because I was too stiff to sit without falling, so that my husband had to tie me to him atop that strange fleshy hump. The heat of the day was punishing and the cold of night, bitter. I spoke almost not at all, for my breathing had become shallow and short. I feared that the paralysis had come to my lungs at last, that I might not make it to the city.

On the third morning, we woke alone in the desert with no water—camel and guide gone—and all but one coin stolen from us.

I could not walk. I could barely breathe. But far on the horizon, my husband said he could see white cliffs, and so he hoisted me into the air, as a bridegroom crossing the threshold with his bride, and began to walk. All that day he walked through the broken desert carrying his wife before him like a cord of wood and the sun beating down. And all that night with the cold stars staring. And more than once he stumbled, but never did he let me fall, and I could do nothing to help but to coax my laboring lungs on, and each breath a trial.

At dawn we came to Velaya.

And having never seen the Dreaming City myself, I could not know with certainty that it had fallen, that it was a husk of its former glory. I had heard only stories of Velaya, and who can say what is fantasy and what is real in a story, no matter how earnest the teller.

But the city was certainly a husk. The Northern Gate was pockmarked; its arches had fallen where their keystones no longer held. The domes of the madrasas which had not collapsed had been stripped of their silver. The streets were dusty and steep and uneven and empty of inhabitants except for a few market-folk in colorless rags selling trinkets and dried nuts from the shadow of low doors.

But my husband entered with his head held high in the dawn light and his eyes stern and his dying bride in his arms.

"We are come to Velaya, my love," he whispered.

And on the blanket of a sun-wizened old rag-picker, from among dirty sandstone idols and chipped crockery, my husband chose a small earthenware jar the size of a hen's egg and traded for it our last coin. And squatting there in the street with myself in his lap—never putting me down—he opened the jar, and with his two fingers scooped from it a gray ointment, and opening my thin black robes, he rubbed the ointment onto my chest.

"A balm of Velaya, my love," he whispered.

And at first I felt only a tingle, but then air rushed into my lungs and I breathed as deeply as a child breathes who wakes from a long and untroubled sleep.

And I would have lain there in his lap breathing and praying and giving thanks —for I had surely been touched by a miracle—but my husband stood with me in his arms, and continued walking up the broken street and in his eyes was a burning intensity. The rag-picker called after us, and some children, ragged also and all skinny, came from the doorways out of curiosity or wonder and followed us on up the street, and more joined, until we were leading some dozens of street urchins in a motley parade. And we wound through the abandoned city until we came, all of us, to a wide plaza with a shallow pool at its center, the pool dry and half-filled with wind-blown sand and its tiles all cracked. Then my husband reached down and grasped a pebble that two of the boys had been kicking and raised it to the light for me to see—a piece of broken cobble with green flecks in its clay—and then he held it to my chest and held me close to *his* chest.

"A stone of Velaya, my love," he whispered.

And as he held me to him, water burst forth in a great arcing spray from the center of the pool and the children all screamed and the mist from the spray of water soaked into our robes and into the rags of the children as they ran and jumped and splashed into the pool. But my husband held me and rubbed more of the ointment into my hands, and as he rubbed the sore useless tendons and the stiff little bones, my fingers returned to life and ached and flexed and clutched his fingers in desperate gratitude. We drank from the pool together, cupping our hands, the clear cold water running down our chins and necks, and rainbows danced in the arcing mist.

There were more shouts as the city-folk came running into the plaza, clapping and ululating and wading in. But my husband lifted me again in his arms, though he did not need to do so for the miracle of the ointment was spreading through my body and I felt my knees tingle and my shoulders and my neck, and a great relaxation came over me, like a fist that has been too long clenched finally unclenching. He walked with me up into the city, through abandoned alleys, past temples, past the eroded faces of old stone gods and the disjoint columns of palaces, and as we walked higher and higher, the wind blew across our wet clothes and the sun warmed us and our skins felt magical. And we climbed up into the cliffs above the city by a long white stair cut from the living rock.

"The Dawn Stair of Veliara, my love," he whispered.

Far below us, from the shoulders of the great cliff, we could see the water from the pool as it shimmered in the sun, and the water overflowed into ancient canals and along aqueducts that had run of old throughout the maze-like city, and the spreading of the new water through the city was as the veins of a leaf held to the sky, except that the veins of Velaya were silver and shining. Then my husband set me carefully down, and though my feet had not felt the ground for some days, I was suffused with a curious lightness, as if I floated like a cork on water. We continued on up the stair, hand-in-hand, always higher, and we were not tired, and we climbed until at last we came to the very summit of Veliara and stood at the cliff-edge looking down into the shining maze of the Dreaming City.

And there was no terror and there was no trial. My husband bent and placed upon that high ground the stone and the small jar of balm and then he took up my hand again. We were not judged. We felt no fear and no uncertainty. We felt no need to leap into the unknown, for we rose from that place on wings we had always known we had.

About the story

"Velaya" was very much inspired by Lord Dunsany, who was a writer of quirky little fantasies in the pre-Tolkien era. I had been fooling around with different voices and styles in my writing, and thought Dunsany's high, Biblical language would be interesting to mimic. Of course, what you set out to do is never quite what you do do, which is true for the protagonist of my story as well.

A question for the author

Q: Are titles easy or hard for you? Do you start with the title or the story?

A: Titles are the best! Really, coming up with titles is like coming up with band names: it's pure id. I usually do it after the fact, with an eye to seeing the title in a list of other titles. Something to stand out, but without, I hope, being too obnoxious.

Chapter titles are even better. When I was revising my (unpublished) novel, *A Catalog of Devils,* I suddenly realized that I could give the 40 or so chapters titles. I went through each chapter, looking for my favorite phrase or word and used that. It was like bringing all the best, trickiest bits of my writing to the forefront. It sounds absurd, but out of the year and a half I spent on the novel, that two hours of titling chapters was the emotional highpoint.

About the author

During the day, Beston Barnett designs and builds furniture in San Diego. At night, he plays Romani jazz. The rest of the time he is reading a book, or eating with chopsticks, or—in the best of all possible worlds —doing both at once.

Switch

Lisa Clark

Claudia Campbell shifted in her seat, clutching her oversized pocketbook closer to her chest. She released an audible huff. With all the automation these days, why couldn't they move things along faster?

She dragged a digital magazine off a nearby table, catching the gaze of another woman. She was probably a decade younger than Claudia's ninety-two, though it was increasingly difficult to tell how old people were these days.

For Claudia, age-retarding pharmaceuticals, surgery, and gene therapy had come too late. She was stuck being old.

She swiped on *Full Life: The Digital Magazine for Seniors* and began flicking through pages filled with ads for precision medications, comfort living, designer foods, cyber companions, etc., etc., etc. *Nothing new here,* she told herself. *Move on.*

Nearby, a man sniffed loudly. With sagging skin, pores the size of pennies, and hound dog jowls, he looked at least a hundred. When he coughed, Claudia could envision micro-flecks of sputum hurtling toward her. She tutted quietly.

Waiting for a doctor today was no more desirable than it had been during the last century. True, the natural light and greenery were pleasant, even if they came courtesy of VR. And the cool aqua-toned seating was attractive and comfortable, with sizes and configurations to fit any patient.

But waiting was still waiting.

She returned to the magazine. On the eighth page, an unbelievably handsome holographic figure popped up. Okay. Claudia would stop to savor a piece of eye candy.

"Ever wonder how it would feel to be someone else?" the man asked in a drawn out, sexy tone. Claudia unconsciously leaned in. "Would it change the way you experience the world or relate to others? Would it make you a better person? At Switch, our VR will take you places beyond your dreams." The hologram looked directly at Claudia. "Come. Try Switch. The world will never look the same."

"Claudia Campbell? Is Claudia Campbell here?" a robotic receptionist called out. Its voice was neither high nor low. Its androgynous body was dressed in blue hospital scrubs. Claudia's lips pursed at its flawless skin.

She pushed herself up. "Yes. I'm here. I've been here for almost an hour."

"Excuse us for the wait," the robot replied, "Physio Caretaker 4 will see you now."

"Hey, Grams," Claudia's grandson called out from the other side of the short wall that separated the living room from the front door. A second later, she heard the *thump* of his satchel as he shoved it onto the seat of the antique hall tree.

Next came a *whump* as Jerrod pushed the door shut against its weatherproofed seal. That sound was Claudia's daily reminder of how much the ranch house had changed since she and Dan bought it back in 1965 as newlyweds. When Jerrod moved in five years ago following the death of his parents, he'd insisted on modernizing.

Claudia strained to greet Jerrod pleasantly. A twenty-eight-year-old had better things to do than spend his life watching over his grandmother, waiting for her to die. The least she could do was welcome him home with a smile.

She was thankful Jerrod didn't treat her like the RoboDoc had earlier. Afterwards, she'd felt like a waste of time, space, and resources. Like the planet would be better off without her.

She'd broken down in the exam room. "My back, my neck, and my joints ache so. It's relentless. Can't you do something? Please! You're supposed to be the best Physio Caretaker in the city."

"Now, Claudia," RoboDoc said.

S/he or it (Claudia never knew how to refer to the unisex care provider) always did that. Called her by her given name.

"First, I'm not the best. Every Physio Caretaker is the same. New models are coming, but we'll all be updated." It tilted its head to the side in a gesture of concern. Claudia wanted to whack the thing over the head with her purse.

"Second, I told you the last three times you were in that your chronic pain is a malfunction in perception. It began with one complaint and, because you didn't deal with that properly, it has continued, spread, and escalated. Your brain is now addicted to the pain. If—"

"Addicted to the pain!" she yelped. "Who programmed you, anyway? People are addicted to things they *enjoy,* at least at the beginning. I have never enjoyed being in pain."

"I'm sorry, but you're mistaken," he answered. Impassively. RoboDocs were infuriatingly emotionless. "As I was about to say, if you continue to feed that addiction, it will continue to grow. My advice? Calm down. Think of something else; occupy your brain with other thoughts and the pain will release its hold on you."

"You know," Claudia stood as indignantly as she could with the nagging cramp in her foot, "back in the days when we had *real* doctors—human ones—they were compassionate. They would have found *some* way to help."

"Back in the days when you had human doctors," RoboDoc answered, "you probably would have been taking fifteen different medicines, none of which would have done a thing besides bankrupt you and interact dangerously with each other." He opened the door. "Don't come to see me again about this issue."

As she rode home in the driverless cab, Claudia brooded. She hated robodocs. Human doctors and nurses could commiserate and touch you with warm skin, assuring you that someone cared.

She had resisted going to the Physio Caretaker because of the cost. Politicians still hadn't figured out how to make medical care affordable and Claudia didn't want to weigh Jerrod down with bills. But he had seen her pain and insisted she go. What a waste.

At home, swirling, grimy, depressing thoughts twined around her. Her hope of relief had shattered. What was left? Maybe it wouldn't be such a bad idea if she scheduled a medical suicide. Plenty of other elderly people did it.

But she was too pathetic, too scared, to take that route.

"Hey, Grams," Jerrod repeated as he rounded the corner into the living room.

Claudia could barely find the strength to meet his gaze.

Seconds later, Jerrod was at her side. "Hey, what's wrong?" His voice was gentle as he knelt by the recliner, her daytime perch for a dozen years. He laid his hand on her shoulder. "What happened? Bad news from the doctor?" His face was still boyish, round, with hair that fell across his forehead and sometimes into his eyes. Their deep blue was so like his grandfather Dan's seventy years ago. She wished Jerrod would wrap her in his arms and draw her close. She ached to inhale his hope.

She shook her head. "No. Not really. Just no help."

His hand slipped onto her wrist. Jerrod was kind. She only wished that, occasionally, he would caress her cheek and hold her hand. But then, her dry, prune-skin face and knobby hands didn't exactly welcome touch.

She shrugged resignation to her fate.

"You know what?" His grin was Dan's. How could she choose medical suicide with this memory of her late husband around? "I have a surprise for you!"

She forced a tiny smile.

"Oh, this will make you a lot happier than that!"

He raced to his room at the end of the hallway, returning less than a minute later.

"Happy birthday!" He bowed smartly at the waist and extended his hand like a butler.

Claudia laughed aloud. "It's not my birthday."

"It will be. In a week. But you need this now."

She eyed the reusable envelope, "guaranteed not to crease, stain, or tear." Claudia was sick of high-tech.

"Open it, Grams. You're gonna love it!" He slid back onto the couch.

She drew out a picture of the unnaturally handsome man she'd seen in hologram form earlier. His words were printed this time. "You are the lucky recipient of a Switch session. Book a time today. After Switch, the world will never look the same."

Claudia didn't look up. She didn't want to see the disappointment in Jerrod's eyes when she refused the gift. She thought he knew her better.

"Great, isn't it?"

"I... Jerrod, I can't do Switch. It's for young people."

"No, no," he protested, slipping onto the couch next to her. "This is for anyone. Everyone. Switch has a great track record, Grams. People up to one-hundred fifteen have entered Switch. Wait a second; I'll call up their testimonials." He slipped on a pair of MR glasses and began manipulating a virtual screen with his fingers.

Claudia pulled his hand down. "Don't bother. I'm not interested. I dislike video games."

"This isn't a game. I've done research on it. I've even talked with Switch clients. No one regrets it."

Claudia grew rigid and clenched her jaw. "Even if you spoke to a hundred people, it means nothing. I'm sure there are just as many with the opposite view. Besides, I've heard about Switch, too. They knock you out with drugs. I don't use drugs. At least, not non-medicinal ones."

"It's not like that. It's more like what they do when you have an operation."

"I don't care to be knocked out!"

"Consider it a nap, then!" He sounded annoyed. "You're always complaining about how you can't sleep."

"It's not the same!" She was yelling now. Her voice sounded like one of those old biddies she used to mock years ago. When had she turned into one of them?

"Listen, Grams." Jerrod stood and loomed over her. "I forked over half a week's salary for this. All I ever hear from you is, 'I can't do this. I can't do that.'" His tone was merciless. "I'm sick of your complaining. All I'm asking is that you give this a try. It's not like you have anything better to do. Can't you think of anyone else for a change?"

Then he marched off to the kitchen.

As Jerrod clanged and clattered dishes and silverware, Claudia doused herself with self-pity, brushing away tears. How could he be so cruel? His grandfather had never acted that way.

No. Not true. Dan regularly had bossed and bullied her around, especially when she resisted him. In the end, she always complied.

She just didn't expect such treatment from Jerrod.

"Dinner's ready." Was that disgust in his voice?

Please, she inwardly begged, *don't be angry with me.* She bit back the urge to cry.

"Coming." Her voice was shaky.

She'd do as he said.

Claudia lay on a gurney in a clean room, her breasts and lower body the only parts covered. Two twenty-something techno-medics worked over her, one a woman with a nametag that read *Tania,* the other a man named *Gopal.* Probably Switch thought they were doing clients a favor by providing human techs. For this, Claudia would have preferred a robot.

She clamped her eyes tight while they glued adhesive sensors to her arms, on skin shriveled like a dried streambed, then to lumpy flesh that sagged into rolls on her stomach. To think, Jerrod had *paid* for this humiliation. Tania and Gopal would probably go home and laugh their heads off at her age-spotted skin.

"So," Tania said, her eyes on the alcohol pad she was swiping Claudia's arm with. "I saw that you chose to enter

Switch as a six-year-old girl. At a birthday party in 1946, right? How fun!"

Claudia didn't want to hear friendly banter. With stinging eyes, she turned from the girl.

"Okay, Mrs. Campbell," Gopal said after the IV was in place. "You're all set. You're in for a fantastic experience."

He settled a mask on her face. "Easy breaths. Now count to ten for me."

Before she reached two, Claudia was out.

"Smile, Louise!" a woman urged.

Claudia-turned-Louise blinked, confused. Where was she? Who was she? Who were these people?

"Smile for the camera, honey!" the woman said.

To Louise, the woman looked like a stranger. Except for her cotton button-up dress with tiny ruffles down the front. And her hair, parted to the side and bobby-pinned away from her face. Around her ears, frizzy curls blossomed. Oh! It was mommy.

A man holding a black metallic cube to his face peeked at her around the box.

"Show me a big six-year-old smile!" His own smile, wide in a thin face, revealed a missing top molar on the left side and another on the bottom right. His white button-up shirt hung large and his belt cinched tightly, creating an elastic-looking waistline. Louise's daddy.

She giggled at her silly confusion and he snapped her. A small *pop* of the flash created a snowy glare in her vision.

Everything was as it should be: a crisp white tablecloth set with good china and silverware. Her baby brother bouncing and slapping his dimpled hands against a highchair tray smeared with smashed peas. Her older brother, wearing a smart plaid suit, honking a noisemaker. Balloons on the table, ruffled sheers on the window, and—Louise reached to make sure—a cardboard crown for her, the birthday girl.

The kitchen door swung open with her grandma singing and carrying a carrot cake decorated with piped rosettes along the top edge and chopped walnuts on the side.

"Blow out the candles and make a wish!" Mommy encouraged.

"Yeah. Hurry up so we can eat cake!" That was her brother.

"I wish I never had to grow up," Louise said.

"Hah! She wants to be Peter Pan!" her brother mocked. "Only now she can't, 'cause she said it out loud."

That bothered Louise as she ate her cake. And again, when she opened her gifts: a pretty dolly whose eyes opened and closed, soft knit slippers, and a red sweater Grandma had knitted with pearly Scottie dogs as buttons.

"Did you have a good birthday, sweetheart?" Mommy asked at bedtime.

"Yes," Louise said. "Except for..."

"Except for what?" Mommy pulled the satiny bedspread up to Louise's chin.

"I don't want to grow up. Now I have to because I said it."

"Not grow up? I thought you wanted to be a mommy."

Louise's brow wrinkled in plump ridges. "I do want to be a mommy."

She woke the next morning with her new doll, a dove cooing outside her window, and a call from downstairs.

"Breakfast!"

The first thing Louise-turned-Claudia noticed as she groggily woke was the odor. A familiar, greasy, old cut-grass scent she couldn't identify.

"Hey, Mrs. Campbell," said an unfamiliar voice. "Welcome back."

Two questions collided in her brain. Why was this stranger urging her from sleep? And where was that disgusting stench coming from?

The woman nudged Claudia's shoulder. "It's time to wake up."

Claudia's eyes fluttered.

"That's it. Welcome back to the world."

Claudia opened her eyes partway. The lights were blinding. And the woman was dressed in white. Had her mother changed her clothes?

Claudia lifted her hand to cover her eyes. They bolted open at the hand coming toward her, shriveled and covered with spots, protruding veins, and swollen knuckles. She lurched upward, only to fall back immediately.

She groaned. Why did her neck feel as though she'd wrenched it?

"No, no." The woman in white—most definitely not Louise's mother—held her down. "Rest a bit. Give yourself time to transition back."

"What? What are you talking about?"

Ten full minutes passed before Claudia's mental fog cleared. Then it all came back, crashing over her like a tsunami.

She was back in the real world.

And that smell? It was her.

"I'll admit I was skeptical about it," Claudia told Jerrod as the taxi whisked them home. The physical contact she'd had inside the program made her crave it again. Why did Jerrod have to sit so far away?

"But you're not now?"

She turned her stiff neck toward him. "It was wonderful to be young again. You have no idea."

He smiled and set his hand on her shoulder. "I'm glad you liked it, Grams."

Her awakening in the clean room after her Switch session didn't return to her fully until the next morning. "Don't worry," the attendant named Destiny had said as she handed Claudia her glasses. "A little confusion is normal, especially after your first session. I'm just glad you're not waking up like the guy last week. Said his whole life had flashed before him." Destiny shook her head. "His Switch session was as a racecar driver. Our medical techs pulled him out of the simulation just before his car crashed. They're very careful to bring people back at any sign of distress. We promise our clients safety, after all." She lifted Claudia's wrist to feel her pulse and nodded a few seconds later. "The only exception was with the guy who signed a waver that said he didn't want to be pulled out early no matter what happened." She leaned forward and said in a hushed voice, "He'd chosen a scenario where he disarmed landmines in a combat zone. He was clearly looking for death by Switch. You know, like people do with police?" Destiny straightened. "The bosses don't allow those types of scenarios anymore."

Claudia often replayed her day in Switch (though, by some computer magic, she knew it had only been an hour in real time). The warmth of her family there. Their closeness. Why had such feelings vaporized in today's world? What was wrong with people these days?

Sometimes, to relive the feel of the red sweater her Switch grandmother had knitted, Claudia closed her eyes and rubbed with withered fingers the afghan draped over her chair arm. But it wasn't the same.

For her birthday, she insisted Jerrod buy her a carrot cake decorated with walnuts.

"*Carrot* cake?" he answered, like she was requesting bugs. "The only kind of cake you'll even touch is dark chocolate."

"I ate it in Switch and have decided that variety is the spice of life."

"All righty, then," he said, holding his hands up in surrender.

She wished she could return to the program to recapture the sensations. To inhale the complex scent of her mother's perfume. Well, Louise's mother.

One day, while Jerrod was at work, Claudia ordered sample vials of fifty vintage perfumes in search of the scent with floral and woody undertones but also powdery and musky. She found it: Lanvin My Sin. One whiff transported her back to the mother that wasn't hers and yet, oddly, had become hers.

"Grams! It smells like an airport duty free shop in here," Jerrod said when he returned home that evening.

She felt like he'd doused her with ditch water.

His brow furrowed. "What?"

She waved him off. How could she explain?

She recalled Louise's downy, unblemished skin and perfect child's body, unmarred by life. Limbs that didn't ache. Eyes that saw without the need of magnification.

As the days passed, Claudia squelched those musings. What a waste of Jerrod's hard-earned money! It was make-believe. If Claudia wanted to pretend, she could read a book or watch TV. That world, that life, that girl—Louise—was merely a construct of computer programmers. How many other people had lived through that exact memory?

Then she remembered. Each Switch scenario was unique; computers designed them based on pre-set parameters, but the program responded to clients' reactions. "When a client acts or speaks, the program goes off in a new direction," the hostess at Switch had explained. "It's never the same, no matter how many people use it."

Which meant the memory of that day and life was Claudia's alone.

Claudia spent most of Thanksgiving Day mourning the family that had been hers for but an hour in the real world.

"What's wrong, Grams?" Jerrod asked.

The lump in her throat made it too difficult to croak out an answer.

She rubbed her throat.

He fetched her lozenges.

The most frightening days—there had only been three—were those when Claudia couldn't stop thinking about reentering Switch. The desire possessed her. Switch could restore to her joy, youth, and connection to people she inexplicably but genuinely loved. She wanted those things so badly she thought her brain might explode if she couldn't have them.

"What's the matter with you, Grams?" Jerrod asked once "You're so irritable."

I'm wishing I could have a life again, she thought. *I'm tired of my body and feeling helpless and useless.*

"Just these old bones getting me down," she said. Her attempted chuckle sounded more like a choke.

"I'm sorry," he said. As though the fault were his. "Work's been crazy. The boss says it should slow down after the holidays. Then I'll be around more."

"I'd like that."

Christmas was near, and Jerrod was feeling guilty about being gone so much. Claudia knew exactly what he could do to assuage his guilt.

"Aren't you going to ask me what I want for Christmas this year?" She pushed aside the lemon cream salmon cannelloni prepared by L'Ultima Chef, Jerrod's favorite kitchen bot. The dish sounded good, but was nothing compared to the home-cooked fare in Switch.

"Ya gotta eat more, Grams," Jerrod grumbled as he scooped up her plate then scraped it into their home composter. When he clicked the button, the machine commenced humming loudly as it began grinding the materials before mixing them into the compost-in-progress. He checked out the temperature inside the device: a bacteria-loving sixty-five degrees Celsius.

Returning to the table, he plunked down. His usually bright eyes were ringed heavily and his face looked drawn. "So, what's this about Christmas? You never have ideas." He ran his fingers through his hair so that it stood straight up for several moments before settling into a style Claudia thought oddly reminiscent of the beehive look of the 1960s. "I haven't had time to think about tomorrow, say nothing of what's coming in two weeks. I'm sorry Grams."

"Don't worry. I've reconciled myself to long periods of isolation." She heaved her shoulders.

Jerrod's face flushed. "Hey, you're not being fair, Grams. This isn't my fault." The deep vertical line between his eyes deepened. It had begun as a shallow depression but had grown more pronounced over the past six months. "How about I check into having a Home Assistant come to spend part of the day with you?" He shook his head miserably. "They're expensive, though."

"I'm not interested in a babysitter!" Claudia snapped.

"How about a senior day care center then?"

"Jerrod Cameron Campbell. *Listen* to me. I'm bringing up Christmas because I have a suggestion for you." Claudia slid her hand across the tabletop. "I wouldn't mind another session at Switch." She made her voice light and nonchalant. "Maybe three hours this time."

Jerrod's jaw dropped.

"You don't have to look so surprised. It's not as though I'm asking you to do something *illegal.*"

"No. I mean, of course not."

"I enjoyed it the first time, that's all." She added softly, "It's hard being old and alone."

"Aw, Grams. I understand." He scraped his fingers through his hair again. "Three hours? Whew. That'll cost a lot." He stared silently at the table for several moments. "Are you sure that's what you want?"

She thrust her chin up. "You're always asking for ideas. Now I'm giving you one."

Jerrod shook his head. "Let me think about it." He pushed himself up from the chair. "I gotta get to bed. I need to be at work early again tomorrow."

Two days after Christmas, at the first opening available, Claudia once again lay nearly naked on a gurney in a clean room while two techno-medics attached electrodes to her skin. She squelched her discomfort. She had forgotten what it felt like to have young eyes look at a body she could barely stand the sight of.

Stop it! a voice inside scolded. *So what if they see you? In a few minutes, you'll be in Switch.*

Claudia couldn't wait to be young again. Not a child, though. This time, she would be living inside the body and mind of a newlywed woman. The time frame she'd chosen was different, too. More suited to an adult. What would it be like, she'd wondered, to assume the life of a new wife after the dawning of the sexual revolution? After men understood they could no longer expect their wives to bow to their every demand? After they saw them as equals?

She had considered the 1960s. Then the 70s. In the end, she'd settled on 1975. There, Claudia could enjoy decent music. She'd grown to dislike almost anything new. Disco had been bad enough, but then came heavy metal. And rap? It was the genre she used to measure all others in terms of horridness. Then came electronic, skewed, and now atomic. Dreadful. All of it.

Uncharacteristically, she'd acted spontaneously and ticked "mystery" on the list of elements she wanted in the program.

Claudia ignored the girl technician's friendly banter, choosing instead to daydream about the scenario she would soon enter.

At first, she'd wanted a groom who would resemble her actual husband, Dan. Then she decided she'd like someone different. Someone like Mel Gibson's character in *Forever Young.*

Switch promised authenticity, not enjoyment. What if she ended up with a chauvinistic bigot like Archie Bunker from that old show, *All in the Family*? She eventually decided that even he must have had some endearing qualities in the beginning.

Besides, anyone Switch matched her to would be exciting; she'd be a newlywed, not someone who'd been married fifty years.

For the dozenth time, Claudia clenched long unused muscles in anticipation.

"Okay, Mrs. Campbell," the male tech said after the IV was in place. "You're ready to enjoy three days of adventure!" His eyes were reassuring. Did Switch only choose employees with pleasant personalities? "When I place the mask on your face, I want you to count to ten. Real easy now."

After "one," she was out.

"I want you to see what I see, Peggy," the man hummed into her ear.

Claudia-turned-Peggy opened her eyes to the reflection of a couple in a full-length mirror. His hair of rich caramel was slicked back. Fawn-colored eyes beneath heavy, straight brows bespoke openness; honesty. Though his face was angular, almost sharp, his lips were full. Exquisite, and somehow more so because they surrounded slightly crooked teeth. His white shirt, opened at the collar, set off tawny skin. In front of him and reaching only to his chin, a somewhat younger woman lifted her gaze. Shy eyes, blue-violet and a trifle too deep-set, contrasted with generous curves beneath a two-piece periwinkle dress, closely fitted. An intricate auburn chignon bared her neck. The cast-iron mirror frame, painted cream and embellished with delicate scallops and intricate vines and leaves, captured the pair like an image in a gallery.

Claudia-turned-Peggy squinted for the briefest moment, trying to place the couple before bursting into a full smile, shaking off the feeling of waking from a dream. This was her, Peggy, with Jack Michaels, the man who had, a few hours ago, promised to be hers and hers alone for as long as they lived.

"Just look at you." Jack stood behind her, wrapping her in his arms. One hand caressed her breast while the other gently pressed and spread over her pubic bone. "You're mine now, Peggy. All and only mine."

She glanced at her own hand, at the finger which held proof that what they were doing was all right. *No. Right.* And *good.* For the first time, she could do what she'd been waiting, wanting to do with this man every day for the past six months. She closed her eyes and leaned back into her husband.

As a railroad shipping clerk and his secretary, Jack and Peggy had meager resources for a fancy honeymoon. "We'll go to San Francisco. Stay in a pretty inn. Eat out a few times. Take in a show, maybe," he'd promised her before their wedding. Which was fine with her. All Peggy wanted was to be with this man.

Soon the mirror, bay window, fireplace, and four-poster bed faded away and there was only Jack and how he was touching her, as though his hands, fingers, and mouth were made for her and nobody else.

Later, barefoot and wrapped in a bedspread that draped behind her like a heavy train, Peggy scampered across the chilly floorboards. Light from a full moon slanted through the tilted blinds, casting the room in stripes of blue-gray. Peggy clicked on a lamp, showering the floor with a wide yellow arc. "We should have started a fire."

For the first time, she noticed a small fruit basket on the table by the window.

"I'll warm you up. Come back to bed." Jack propped himself up on an elbow.

"Jack! I'm hungry."

"I am, too." He twitched his brows Groucho Marx-style.

Peggy bit into a green apple. "This is so nice. Do they leave fruit for everyone, or just for newlyweds? Oh, wait. Here's a card."

With apple still in hand, she broke the envelope's seal. A moment later, the apple rolled down the bedspread and *thunked* onto the bare floor. The covering slid to her waist and her face twisted in confusion.

"What?" Jack threw back the blanket and padded toward her.

Peggy barely noticed that he was naked. That the skin along one of his sides was peppered with dozens of maroon scars. That he was ready for her again.

"What's wrong?" He wrapped one arm around her and grabbed the card with the other.

Johnny, it said, *Your new wife very pretty, but she know about Linh and Johnny Jr.?*

Jack froze.

"Jack?"

"This is a mistake." He released her to rip the card and toss it into the fireplace. "It has to be. Who's Johnny? And who's Lin? Or however you say that name. Get back in bed, Peggy, and I'll build a fire."

"But—"

"It's mis*take,* honey. Trust me." The way he kissed her, carried her to the bed, and made love to her again made Peggy almost forget the note.

Later, when they left for dinner, Jack slid the fruit basket onto the reception desk. "There's been an error," he said. "This is someone else's."

"But, sir," the manager protested, "someone left it specifically for you,".

"It's not ours."

*

The next morning, Peggy spotted a bakery and Jack a fruit cart at the same time. "Let's surprise each other," she suggested. "You buy fruit. I'll buy pastries."

"Perfect," he agreed. "We can eat in the park."

The selection of freshly made breads and doughnuts kept Peggy in the shop longer than she'd planned.

Finally, balancing a rough cardboard holder for their coffee cups in one hand and a box with enough treats for three days in the other, she swiveled to exit.

Through the window, she spotted Jack with a strange woman.

The small bell above the door tinkled as she pushed it with her shoulder. Jack, several feet away, shot her a glance then hissed something to the woman.

The stranger—some sort of Oriental, Peggy thought—peeked around Jack and sneered at her with such venom that Peggy gasped. The coffee holder wobbled precariously in her hand.

"... sister know... you... must care..." The woman's voice was harsh but indistinct.

As Peggy warily approached, the stranger bustled away, weaving through pedestrians, hustling to their daily grinds.

"Who was that?"

Jack shook his head. "Just a beggar. There are lots of them here."

"But what did she say? Why were you talking to her?"

Jack goggled at Peggy as though she'd accused him of a crime.

"I-I mean," she stuttered, "I was just wondering."

He smiled, but not warmly, then pressed on the small of her back a touch too firmly. "Let's go and eat."

*

Jack was wonderful, mostly, for the rest of the day, and possessive and intense that night. "I love you so much, Peggy. You. Only you," he told her two, three, four times.

Her timid, "I love you, too, Jack," after the last time brought him to tears, though he tried to hide it.

"You're mine and I'm yours. No one else's," were his last words that night.

*

The sights as they hopped off the trolley the next day—signs featuring "imperial," "Chinese," and hanzi characters alongside tall buildings topped with pagodalike roofs—made Peggy glad her aunt had suggested Chinatown. Here they'd find coconut buns, egg yolk almond balls, mooncakes, and who knew what else.

The air vibrated differently here. The fragrance of unfamiliar spices wafted from shops and mixed with crisp, precise music with odd rhythms.

Tomorrow they would drive home. The next day, it was back to work.

Peggy didn't want to miss a thing.

Outside the Far East Café, she decided to use the restroom. "Find a shop we can visit," she said. "I'll be quick."

When she reemerged, Jack wasn't waiting by the door. She scanned the sidewalk to her right, then to her left. No sign of him. Her stomach clenched. What if she couldn't find him?

But that was silly. Jack would never leave her.

She gazed across the street, in the direction of Fisherman's Wharf, already bustling. After a jangling trolley passed, she spotted Jack. Again, with another woman. Was it the one from yesterday? He extracted the wallet from his pocket, glanced nervously around, then handed the woman money.

What was he *doing*? Why was he with her? And why was he giving her money?

Peggy stepped off the curb onto the street, furious, aware of nothing but Jack.

A horn blared at her.

Peggy screamed.

A car screeched, then plowed into her, throwing her to the ground.

The driver jumped out and cursed her. People stopped to watch.

The next moment, Jack was there.

And then he wasn't. Peggy-Claudia was out of Switch.

"Hey, good morning, Grams!" Jerrod clicked off the burner and pivoted from the stovetop, where he was whipping up his favorite weekend concoction: scrambled eggs with garlic, scallions, and jalapenos.

He flicked off the virtual comp display on the table, opened to the news.

"How did your Switch session go?" he asked as she settled into her chair. "I peeked in on you last night when I got home, around nine, but you were already asleep."

"It was good."

"Good. That's great. Would you like some eggs?" He scooped his breakfast onto his plate.

"With hot peppers? No thank you."

"I can make the kind you like."

"No, no, sit." She tapped the table with her fingers, noticing how gnarled they were. So different from yesterday, inside Switch.

Why did she have to return? To wake every day in a ninety-two-year-old body? To constant swollen ankles. To teary eyes. To hauling one leg over the other with both hands, as though performing a herculean chore. To shriveling skin and the inability to stand erect.

Her shuffle down the hallway seemed a trifle longer every day.

What did life offer her besides more pain, more loneliness, and more hopelessness?

Switch delivered her from all that. Her brain stored Switch experiences just like real ones. In fact, memories from Switch were fresher and clearer. That didn't mean she forgot actual people and events from her past. But her Switch family as a child... Her marriage to Jack... How he reinvigorated sensations in this old body of hers... It was squirmingly delightful.

The truth? Claudia had been awake last night when Jerrod came to her door. She'd been reliving Jack's breath on her cheek and neck. His fingers on her skin. The way he possessed her.

Dan had never made her feel like that.

Jerrod handed her a mug of coffee with a splash of coconut milk. "So, tell me about your adventure."

"It was... lovely." She almost cringed. She sounded like such an old lady.

He chuckled and slapped his palm onto the table playfully. "Come *on*, Grams. Details, please."

Claudia felt her face redden and lifted the mug to her mouth. She couldn't remember the last time she'd blushed and that thought almost made her blush again. She sucked in a breath. "Okaaaay. This time I visited San Francisco in 1975."

Jerrod nearly choked on a mouthful of juice. "Are you kidding? I'd love to see Frisco before the earthquake and wildfires destroyed so much of it."

"So, take some time off work."

"Grams," he groaned.

She waved a hand at him that resembled a bundle of twigs.

"What did you do there?"

Hmm. What was she supposed to say? That she had enjoyed the thrill of first-time sex for the second time in her life? About being smitten with Jack? No. Definitely not. She'd improvise.

"I met a young man. And his wife. Newlyweds." She leaned into the table edge, flattening her saggy breasts. "They were lodging in the same guesthouse, and —"

"Oh. What was the guesthouse like?"

"Lovely, dear, but that wasn't the interesting part."

Jerrod rose to clear his plate. "More coffee?"

"Not yet."

He refilled his mug and resettled onto his chair. "You were saying?"

"Well, this husband—we'll call him Jack. And his wife, Peggy."

"What was your name?"

What? Claudia fumbled for a second. "Jill. I was Jill."

"Ha! You shoulda been married to the guy. Jack and Jill. Funny."

Claudia's face warmed again. "Are you going to talk or listen?"

"Geez, Grams. Go on."

Claudia told about the fruit basket, Jack's reaction to it, the whispering woman, and finally the money exchange.

"What were you, a spy? How did you find out about all that?"

"I, um, Jill, I mean Peggy, was my sister. She told me."

"You didn't say you were sisters."

Claudia huffed. "It's a *story*, Jerrod. That's all. I'm just trying to figure out why Jack was hiding information about the woman from his new wife."

Jerrod's eyes narrowed. "I have a feeling you're not telling me everything."

Claudia threw her napkin at him.

"Okay, okay. Maybe he was a Vietnam War vet. The time was right. Maybe the strange woman was Vietnamese, not Chinese. The sister of a woman Jack had met in Vietnam. Maybe they married and had a son. 'Johnny' could be a nickname for 'Jack.' That would fit. When the war ended, Jack had to leave the country, his wife, and his child."

Claudia stared at him. "That must be it." Her brow furrowed. "Jack had another wife."

Jerrod shrugged. "Don't be too hard on the guy. Soldiers get lonely during wartime."

Claudia sighed. "That's true." She pushed herself up from the chair.

"Wait, Grams. Aren't you going to eat?"

She swung her hand behind her. "I'm fine."

But she wasn't fine. Imagining Jack with another woman shook Claudia. Why hadn't he said anything? She would have understood.

She thought she would, anyway.

Halfway to her room, she froze. Jack was not her husband. Not really. He had been a character in a computer simulation. That's all.

Claudia slumped against the wall. *But it's not all. Jack was my husband. Those things happened. They were real.*

By the end of the day, one thought pummeled her: she had to return to Switch, to Jack. She couldn't bear never seeing him again.

"I'm sorry, Ms. Campbell," the woman said. On the virtual screen, she looked pleasant enough, but she was inflexible as a broomstick. "What you're asking for is impossible."

These people had promised a customized experience. Why were they now unwilling to keep that promise?

"Our programs are not reproducible," the woman went on. "I'm sure someone told you that. To work within program parameters, our technology cannot recreate the kind of details you want."

Claudia's shoulders drooped. She did remember that. "You mean," she asked in a tiny voice, "I'll never be able to go back to my husband?"

"Your husband?"

"I mean, my Switch husband."

"Oh. No. I'm sorry." Later, this woman would probably laugh at Claudia for believing in the world and life Switch had created for her. Right now, she sounded compassionate. "Please allow me to make up for the confusion. I can offer you a special deal: one week inside of Switch for the price of four days. You can choose a program similar to the last, if you like. How does that sound?"

It would have to do. "Okay. Mark me down for a week from today."

As she disconnected, the awful truth washed over Claudia. She'd never see

Jack again. Never inhale his Old Spice. Or lie by his side. She'd never find out his secret—or tell him she forgave him for keeping it from her. And her lips would never feel his again.

She touched her lips with her fingers, closed her eyes, and saw Jack's kind face. He seemed to be speaking to her. Telling her to move on.

Could she? If she married again, it wouldn't be as though she'd *lose* Jack. He was in there to stay.

Over the next hours, Claudia's mind created a new wish list for her next Switch session. This time, she'd visit a later timeframe: the 2010s. She wouldn't tick off "mystery" in the story elements. She hated not knowing—never knowing—the truth about the Asian woman. Jerrod might have been right in his conjecture, but he might also have been wrong.

This time... This time... Ohhhhh. Yes! This time, she'd spend her honeymoon in Paris. And *this* time, she would opt for a man with an "intriguing" side to his character. She clenched the muscles she would use to satisfy her new husband and laughed out loud.

Instantly, she slapped her hand over her mouth, forgetting for a moment that

Jerrod was at work. Then she laughed again. She could fantasize as much as she liked.

By the end of the day, she had only one problem: where would the money come from? The session would cost a full month of Jerrod's pay and he'd never agree to taking out a loan. She'd figure something out.

"Grams, you're awfully chipper tonight," Jerrod said at least four times that evening. The last time, he followed the comment with, "So, are you going to let me in on your secret?"

No. Absolutely not. The poor boy would probably die of shock. "I'm just happy, that's all."

The next evening, the door clicked open. Jerrod stepped in. "Hey G—" Silence reigned for two seconds. "What?" Five seconds more, and he was around the corner, staring at her.

Claudia glanced up from the electronic book she'd been reading. A trashy romance—the kind she used to consider obscene. Now, it fueled her imagination.

The line between his eyes deepened as Jerrod fisted the hair at the top of his head. "What happened to the hall tree?"

Claudia had expected this. "Well, hello to you, too, dear."

He slipped out of his sleek winter jacket and held it in one hand, letting it drape to the floor as his gaze fixed on her.

They make everything so lightweight these days, Claudia thought, blinking. When she was a child, she remembered piling on so many layers she'd end up clomping around like Frankenstein.

She swiped her book close.

"Where is it, Grams?"

Her shoulders lifted slightly then dropped as she sighed. "I sold it."

"What?" The jacket slipped from Jerrod's fingers.

"I sold it. It was a monstrosity. Besides, it didn't fit in with the rest of our furnishings. You know that. It was old."

Jerrod collapsed onto an easy chair. "I can't believe you did that. *Why?* What were you *thinking*?"

Claudia shrugged and turned instead toward the front window. It was dirty, streaked and splotchy from bugs and rain. She'd noticed that earlier, as the sun set. When had it last been cleaned? Years ago.

She never would have let that happen in her younger years.

"Grams!"

The sharpness of his tone made her jerk. She twined her fingers together like grapevines coiled into a wreath.

"That was mine! You know that. Just because it didn't come from your side of the family doesn't mean it wasn't valuable to me. It was the only thing I had of Dad's grandparents."

She shrugged again. "It was ugly, Jerrod. The mirror was blackened in the corners. And those claws meant to hang coats on? There were ridiculous."

"It was an antique! If the piece were restored, it could have sold for more than this house is worth."

"Maybe. But it wasn't restored," she snapped. "I was sick of looking at it."

"So what? I put up with this dust-infused living room set of yours. You don't even sit on it! You perch yourself in that La-Z-Boy like it's some kind of throne."

Claudia supposed he didn't mean to sound so nasty. Still, his words hurt.

After a long pause, she mumbled, "Buy something modern instead. Something you'll enjoy."

"I en*joyed* that. It gave me a connection to the past. Now, tell me what you did with it so I can get it back."

Claudia barked out a laugh. "I have no idea who the buyer was. He didn't leave his name or contact information. I'm sorry."

Jerrod pounded the arm of the chair, sending up a thin mist of dust. "You're not sorry at all!" He bolted out of the chair, swiped his jacket off the floor, glanced around as though trying to find something, then threw it back down. With his back toward her, he said, "You still haven't told me why."

Claudia fiddled with the edge of the arm cover on her chair. It was old, like her, and frayed. Not good for much. "I needed the money," she said, her voice only barely above a whisper.

"What?" He turned slowly.

His tone flipped something inside of Claudia.

"I said I needed the money." Now her voice was defiant.

"For *what?*"

"For returning to Switch, if you must know."

He gaped at her. "You just *had* a session at Switch."

"Well I need to go again. The woman offered me a great deal: a week for the price of four days. I couldn't pass it up. I've already booked a session for next Monday."

Jerrod's head flinched back. "You're going for a *week*? How long is that in Switch time?"

"Roughly six months."

"*Six months?* Are you crazy? Why?"

She swung her head to the side. "You wouldn't understand."

Jerrod said nothing for a long time, but she could feel him gaping. As though she'd just grown horns. Then, shaking his head slowly, he said, "Okay. I won't stop you. Just don't sell any more of my stuff."

That evening, Jerrod ate in his bedroom, Claudia in her La-Z-Boy.

I'll make it up to him, Claudia vowed to herself before drifting off that night.

When Claudia emerged from her week-long Switch session, her eyes sprang open and she surveyed the wake-up room. Within a half a minute, she understood who she was, what the thirty-something male watching over her was doing, and that she was out of the program. Safe.

"Whoa there, Mrs. Campbell," the man said as she jostled to raise herself up on her elbows.

Cursed old age. It was a bother more than anything. There were more important things to do in life than sit around, watching other people live. That's what Damian, her Switch husband for the last six months, used to say. For several moments, the room and attendant vanished as Damian's image filled her inner vision: movie star handsome, dressed in edgy haute couture, holding a champagne glass. And there she was—as Rosa—by his side. Also beautiful. Also dressed in the latest fashion and firmly ensconced in the high life. Wearing a three-carat blue diamond ring, studded with twists of black and white diamonds.

The attendant gentled Claudia onto her back. "Give yourself a little time to readjust. No one's chasing you, you know."

But they were!

Or, they had been. Since Rosa and Damian's honeymoon in Paris, life had become a game of cat and mouse with INTERPOL.

On their wedding night, Rosa had learned that Damian was a fraud artiste (he loved calling himself that; "con man" was too plebeian) and lived luxuriously by scamming people. He mixed both targets and methods frequently to avoid capture. Damian concealed his occupation from friends by claiming to be the obscenely rich heir of a powerful Bulgarian family.

At first, Rosa was horrified. After seeing Damian in action, though, she slowly warmed to his tricks. Soon, she joined him.

The law, never far behind, provided an unending source of adventure.

Their lives together vaporized when she reemerged from Switch.

How could she bear to return to her mundane reality, sitting around, waiting to die?

"Well, your vitals look remarkably good for someone who's been in an induced coma for a week. How do you feel?"

Miserable, she thought. "As well as a ninety-two-year-old can expect, I suppose."

"Excellent!"

"Grams, what's the matter?" Jerrod helped her sit up against the headboard and set a decades-old breakfast-in-bed tray in front of her.

Her lip curled at the black metal surface, decorated with a painted floral design, long-ago faded. Years of dust, miniscule crumbs, and spilled liquids, never thoroughly cleaned from its crevices, made it slightly tacky and thoroughly gross. They should have thrown it out long ago. How could she ever have thought such a cheap, unsophisticated item was charming?

For that matter, how had she lived so long in such an unattractive home, surrounded by things Damian and Rosa would have scorned? The high life was the only life for the person Claudia had become.

She stared at the Saturday morning meal her grandson had prepared for her: a poached egg, fruit bowl, fresh croissant, and steaming mug of coffee. "It looks wonderful, dear." Her voice sounded as bereft of enthusiasm as she felt.

Jerrod scooted the table over a bit and sat on the edge of her bed. She hadn't laundered the sheets, hadn't even changed out of her nightgown for a week. Since her return from Switch.

She must reek. But what difference did it make?

Nothing appealed to her anymore. She dreaded the thought of beginning each day in her drab bedroom, on this old-fashioned bed. Dreaded opening her eyes to another chapter of boredom and pain.

Switch was all she wanted, all she craved. The only thing that could satisfy her.

Jerrod cocked his head to the side and lifted her shriveled hand. *No, that thing isn't a hand; it's a jumble of bones,* she thought. She wiped the corners of her eyes, pretending to be doing what she needed to do dozens of times daily because of her annoying runny eyes.

She was so sick of life.

"I blame myself for your... What is it, Grams? Depression? You haven't been the same since you returned from Switch. You're wasting away. Sometimes I think a stranger has taken over my grandmother's body. What did they do to you?" He was growing agitated. Angry. "Or was the program they plugged you into upsetting? Please! You haven't told me anything."

She smiled at him. Sadly. How could she tell her grandson that she'd embraced a life of crime with a handsome man who was more exciting, more alive than anyone she'd known in real life? That all she wanted was to return to him, knowing she never could?

Jerrod would never agree to fund another Switch session for her. In a way, he *was* responsible for her current state. It was no use telling him that, though. He wouldn't understand.

Claudia's mind flung back to the scene on Rosa and Damian's wedding night as they strolled along a tiny Paris street, alive with bistros and brasseries, toward one of the city's most elegant restaurants.

"Wait here," Damian had told Rosa, who was too surprised to object.

He trotted a half block ahead of her, looking like a model in his well-fitted suit. After crossing the street, he wove around passersby until he reached the sidewalk seating area of a bistro. At the first table, he smiled and, in perfect French, asked if the couple was enjoying their meal. "Oui, oui monsieur," they answered. He bowed his head and moved on to two other tables.

At the third, the dining couple had yet to pay the bill, left in a guest check book on their table. "I hope madam and monsieur were satisfied with their meal and service." "Oui, oui." "Excellent. I'll take this for you." Within three minutes, Damian was at her side again with the man's credit card in his pocket, several hundred meters beyond the restaurant.

Rosa had been mortified.

Damian slowly wore down her objections. "I never hurt anyone," he assured her. To prove it, after paying for their dinner with the stolen card, Damian melted it.

The second scam didn't seem quite as bad to her.

Soon, Rosa was helping Damian conjure up ways to defraud people. Neither of them wanted to destroy people's lives. Their goal was to pilfer only the money people would have wasted anyway.

"I... I'm sorry to worry you, dear," Claudia told Jerrod now. "I'll be okay. Just give me a little time."

Claudia had considered several ways to take money from Jerrod. Scruples weren't the problem; she mainly feared being caught. Plus, well, he *was* her grandson.

It wasn't until that evening, exactly seven days after her return, that Claudia figured out how to reenter Switch. This time, she'd order the longest session available. And she wasn't going to waste it on a quotidian scenario. This time, she'd *really* live.

Again she lay on a gurney in a clean room while two techs bustled around, attaching sensors to her nearly naked form.

She focused on the program ahead. She'd opted for the year 2030, when regular people began skydiving from the edge of space. She'd chosen the program because of its risks, but thinking about them now scared her. She squeezed her eyes tightly.

"Everything all right, Mrs. Campbell?" the young woman asked.

She was *going* to do this. "Yes, I'm okay."

"Almost there," the young man said. Months ago, Claudia would have considered him a boy. That was before she married Jack and Damian.

She shifted her gaze to the wall and again her thoughts raced. Did she really want this? She could be facing a puncture in her jump suit that would create gas bubbles in her bodily fluids. Her blood would literally boil. Or she could end up in a flat spin that would whip her around up to 250 rotations a minute, stealing her breath away or even bursting her eyeballs. A collision or blackout could also take her life.

Actually, a blackout didn't seem so bad. That would be okay.

She hated leaving Jerrod with no explanation. At least she'd met him in the hallway that morning, rising to wish him a good day—a good life, really, though she couldn't say that without alerting him to her plan. She'd set her left hand on his arm. "Don't worry about me, Jerrod. I'll be fine." Thankfully, he didn't register the absence of her wedding ring. Before she sold it, she hadn't taken it off since her wedding day. With the money, she bought a two-week session, which meant a year inside Switch.

"Okay, then," the young woman said. "You're all set."

Claudia inhaled deeply.

"Hope this is your best experience yet." The woman settled the mask on Claudia's face. "Please count to ten for me."

Claudia-turned-Rochelle's eyes opened slowly, as though awakening after a long sleep. After half a second, they popped wide, like a goby fish. Her lips parted to scream, but something was clamped over her mouth, her nose, her chin. Even pulling her head back was impossible.

"Hey, Rochelle. Everything okay?"

Who was Rochelle? And why was a man's voice inside her head? Her focus turned from the visor in front of her face to the view outside. Her heart stopped, or skipped a few beats, or did something else abnormal, because the voice was back.

"Rochelle! Speak to me."

She shut her eyes to block the panorama beyond her face mask: the curvature of Earth; its azure painted with cloudy swirls.

Then her mind cleared. "Um, yeah Phil. I'm fine. I was disoriented for a second. I'm all right now."

Phil was twenty-two-year-old Rochelle Moreau's jump team leader on this, her first dive from near space. This suit, the helmet, visor, gloves, and special boots were her protection from one of the planet's most dangerous climates.

"You're falling at four hundred miles per hour already."

"Cool."

Phil's staccato *ha-ha-ha*s made her smile.

Despite her speed, Rochell's jump—which she remembered now had begun at 135,000 feet above the Earth—felt calm.

"You're up to 600 mph now," Phil said a short time later.

Now Rochelle laughed. This was amazing. She shifted her orientation with a slight movement. During freefalls at lower altitudes, this was easy. Out here, so far from the Earth's surface, it felt different. Her throat constricted at the passing thought of being stranded in space. That was impossible; she wasn't out nearly far enough.

As she plummeted, Rochelle could make out mountains and large bodies of water.

She jostled to the right to try to identify a shape, then something went wrong. An invisible force shoved her. The next moment, she was spinning. No, no, *no*. This was bad. Very bad. If she didn't get herself under control, she'd soon be nothing but sausage in a fancy coat, splatting onto the frying pan of the New Mexican desert floor.

Fear enveloped her. How many rotations a minute was she up to?

"Push against the spin, Rochelle!"

I can't, she thought. *I'm gonna die up here.*

"Spread your arms and legs into a layout position," Phil barked. "Do it now!"

Rochelle obeyed. Almost instantly, her spinning slowed. Soon, the ground was in focus again.

Good thing Phil was such a hard-ass.

She heard him exhale.

"How fast am I going?" Her record before was 500 mph.

"You've reached 800 mph."

She wanted to laugh. Spread-eagle, she spotted fields and rivers below. Then buildings and roads came into focus.

"You're at four minutes, Rochelle. Ten thousand feet. Time to open the chute."

The sudden yank, which always felt gentle at lower altitudes, felt like a punch after freefalling for so long.

Soon, the toe of Rochelle's right boot touched down. She loped clumsily for ten gigantic steps, then threw her arms into the air before falling onto her knees, crying.

She had to do this again.

At the completion of twenty-five successful jumps, Rochelle became a record-holder in the world of space-chuting. By then, she felt invincible.

On her twenty-sixth jump, 363 days after her first, Rochelle Moreau slammed into a flock of migrating Greater Sandhill Cranes at 6,000 feet.

She did not survive.

About the story

"Switch" came to me as a sort of spin-off of the YA SF novel I'm working on called Skin Changers. In that book, teens are the ones to the immersive VR program. Its purpose is to help them grow in empathy.

But what if old people - people like Claudia in "Switch," who grew up before the age of computers - could enter that type of program? What scenarios would they choose? How would it change them? Would reentering "life" again as young people become addictive? So many questions could be explored. Some, in pain and without hope of for a better personal future like Claudia, might use the program as a final solution to their desperation.

A question for the author

Q: What five words describe you?

A: creative, organized, quiet, purposeful, and thoughtful

About the author

If Lisa Clark could enter a program like Switch, she'd go 1) back to Israel 1,999 years ago (but her avatar would have to know the local languages) 2) a thousand years back to sit on Mauna Kea Hawaii to stargaze 3) back to see herself as a teenager (though she's not sure they'd allow that). While waiting for that tech to be developed, she'll try to make the best of the world we've got.

lisakclark.com

The Three Sisters

Keith Azariah-Kribbs

Once upon a time there were three brothers who lived with their parents in the midst of a vast forest. If there were any other people in the forest, they knew nothing of them, for they found no trails other than those they themselves had blazed, and they found no pits for iron in the bogs other than those they themselves had dug, and they discovered no hewn trees other than those they themselves had hewn.

The three young men grew well in the midst of this forest until they had mastered their trades and wanted for nothing. For none could track or hunt or cure hides and weave cloth so well as Wulfstan, and none could forge iron or steel or fire molded clay into vessels so well as Odduin, and none could better coax the barley or the flax from the fields or encourage the ash trees to produce fairer and straighter limbs than Baldry. In their skills they were masters, and their home was filled with carved wood and stone and with jewels and wrought gold and silver the envy of any prince. Other skills they had and shared, but in these, they each were alone the master. But they knew nothing of that, for they supposed themselves alone in the world.

As their lives could not have been bettered with company, it never occurred to the three brothers to wonder why there were no other people in the world. It was just so.

Yet the world could become lonelier still, and the day dawned when the father and mother of Wulfstan, Odduin, and Baldry died. The three brothers found them thus in their bed after the long cool of the night of the autumnal equinox, and straightway prepared for them a suitable burial.

Baldry carved a coffin out of a single great branch of a favorite oak, Odduin forged golden hasps, hinges, and handles for the coffin, and Wulfstan fashioned a princely cloak of silver ferrel fur underlain by fine linen and with a clasp of gold adorned with emeralds for their coverlet. And then they placed the coffin to float on the river, and they stood by the bank and watched at twilight until the current carried the coffin so far to the south that the corpse candles over the coffin could no longer be seen in the gathering gloom.

With that, the brothers felt a strange chill fall on their broad shoulders as the dusk descended, and each turned silently to his workshop, but they could not busy themselves with their craft, and instead they sat and wondered at how dark and empty the world suddenly seemed.

For a time and half a time, the three brothers mourned as is fitting, but eventually they decided that the time for mourning was past. And as the strange gloom that had fallen on them had not eased, they took council among themselves.

Odduin, who was regarded as the wisest of the three, gathered his brothers beside the glowing fire of his forge and the warmth of his kiln, and he spoke. "Brothers, we are alone now in the world, and the warmth we had of our family has gone. I can find no joy in my work, for now there is none to take delight in it, no mother to make her presents of golden combs or father to make him gifts of iron tools."

Baldry nodded in agreement. "So it is, brother. What shall I do now with the carved seat I intended for our mother for Yule, or the barley ale I brewed for our father's table?"

"I could make use of that barley ale, if you're truly stuck with it," Wulfstan whispered. "But you're right, brothers. My fine shawls and gowns for our mother— I'm afraid we are going to look very foolish wearing them."

Odduin frowned at his brother, and Baldry laughed, but silently.

"And that is why men marry," Wulfstan declared. "So that they will have someone to please with presents of gold and silks and gems. We must marry."

"But we no longer have mother and father to find us suitable wives," Baldry said.

"And so we must look to this task ourselves," Odduin declared.

"How can we, brother?" Wulfstan replied, "Seeing there are no others in all this great forest wherein we alone wander?"

"We must go beyond the forest, Wulfstan, and seek wives in the wider world. For our father found a wife in this world, unless we are to believe he fashioned her himself out of the clay of the bank or the iron of the bog or the wood of the forest. I will seek to the north, toward the mountains of ice under the pole star. Wulfstan, you shall seek to the west, toward the plains under the setting sun. And you, Baldry, shall seek to the east, toward the hills under the rising sun. We need not search to the south, for we know well that the great forest there is the haunt of demons and dragons and trolls, and we will find no women there."

"Unless there be one there who could daunt demons and dragons and trolls, and she would make a fine, blushing bride, I'd wager," said Wulfstan.

Odduin stood. "For two moons of Islith shall we walk, and then we will return here and we shall know where we are to find our wives."

And so it came to pass. In the morning, Odduin banked the great fire in his forge and closed the flue on his great kiln, Wulfstan set the last of his hides to dry on the racks and doused the fires in his smokehouse and rolled up his great bolts of fine linen, and Baldry harvested the last of the year's grain into his barn and placed a bung in his beer barrel, and then each brother bade the others farewell and they set out.

The moons of Islith passed quickly enough, and at twilight of the last day of the fourth moon, the three brothers stepped from the forest into the clearing alone, and each nodded to the others in mute acknowledgment of the failure of the quest.

Odduin kindled the fires in his forge and his kiln, but he simply sat beside the fire and gazed into its ruddy glow. Wulfstan took up his bow and stepped into the forest to hunt, but he simply sat on a fallen log in the glade until the night's dew covered his shoulders. And Baldry opened his barn, inspected the harvest for mice, and noted that his beer had fermented properly during his absence, though he did not bother to fetch down a mug for himself or his brothers.

The next morning, the three brothers met at the long table and took council.

"Brothers," Odduin said, "In all my wandering I found no women in all the world. I see it is the same with you, Wulfstan, and also with you, Baldry."

"Yet our father had a wife," Baldry observed.

"Even so. It may be that in some way he fashioned her himself. Therefore I propose, brothers, that we do this thing out of our craft. For my part, I am a master of iron and clay. I will set to this task tomorrow morning. I advise you to do likewise. See here. I have returned with the sacred waters taken from the well of Uldar at the foot of the mountains of ice, guarded by the nymphs. It may be that this water will bring life to iron and clay and wood and stone and hide, if we but fashion a suitable vessel to contain it. But be warned, for the nymphs, grudging my taking of their water, warned me that although this water brings life, so also does it assure strife and pain."

"Strife and pain come to all that live, brother," Baldry said. "Except to the nymphs of the well of Uldar. We shall attempt this task."

And so the next morning Odduin set the clay to fire in the kiln and the iron to heat in the forge. Wulfstan took his finest furs and his softest cloth and began to stitch them together, and Baldry began to carve the finest wood, after settling on rowan for his beloved. Into the working of their materials, the brothers mingled the waters stolen from the well of Uldar. And after laboring until dusk on this work, each brother left to take his rest. And so they continued for many days.

Now, it was unfortunate, if understandable, that the brothers had avoided searching the demon and dragon and troll haunted forest to the south, for had they done 'so, they might have discovered the mighty city of Ib that lay below the great forest. In this evil city there are many women, though few of them honest enough to wed, and many men as well, though few of them suited for much other than craft and intrigue.

The citizens of this city were likewise afraid of the great forest to the north, knowing it to be the haunt of terrible fiends that delighted to rend the flesh of city people particularly. Yet they coveted the lumber of this forest, which they dared not cut. Instead, they gleaned whatever logs floated down the river from time to time, regarding them as gifts from the gods, and the gods were especially generous after the great storms descended from the ice mountains in the far north. And the people of Ib coveted the gold and gems that they found in the gravels and sands along the banks of the river, washed down from hidden veins of untold riches somewhere in that forest.

Thus the people of Ib spent many hours in the reaches of the river just above the city, collecting goods with which to barter or to fashion their cruel idols and elegant seats of power. And so it came to pass that Freydor, the fisher, who cast his nets into the waters of the river just above the city and had occasionally fished as much as a furlong upstream into the forest, though remaining watchful for demons and dragons and trolls along the banks, found the drifting casket containing the remains of the three brothers' parents.

Freydor was astonished at the quality of the casket, the elegantly carved and polished oak wood, each end of the casket decorated with the likeness of a dragon's head, the sides of the vessel adorned with beautiful nymph's faces and terrible wolves, alternating down the sides of the casket. He marveled at the quality of the gold hinges and hasps, each in the shape of a great lion's paw, and he thrilled at the sight of the coverlet, the ferrel furs finer than those worn by the corrupt Prince Ladlow, the linen suitable for Princess Asriel's shift, and the golden clasp, wrought in the likeness of an angel with inlaid silver and crusted with emeralds, more magnificent than the crown that sat atop the dissipated brow of King Durac himself.

Freydor was a craftsman of some repute, but he acknowledged that the men who fashioned this vessel were his masters. And he divined that three separate hands had been at work here, one on the wood, another on the gold, and yet a third on the furs and fabrics.

Now, three was a number of some interest to Freydor, for he had three daughters of surpassing loveliness, and he was loath to see them wed to mere tradesmen of the city of Ib. For the men of Ib were grasping, thoughtless, frivolous creatures, and they required of their women both stature and wealth or they would not take them to wife. Yet Freydor fancied his daughters as far above the noble women of Ib as the soaring hawk is above the humble, if practical, kingfisher. Moreover, Freydor knew his daughters for honest women, and he would not see them bound to the worshippers of the lying god Yerolka, who was currently fashionable in Ib and who gave men mastery over their wives in measure beyond their desert, and who encouraged women to cultivate deceit as their revenge for this abuse.

Thus Freydor pondered this matter deeply for some hours. Then, just as the sun touched the western horizon, he devised his plan to send his daughters to wed these unknown craftsmen. Such men were obviously unwed, for no wife of Ib would approve such an extravagance as this coffin, and they must surely match his daughters well, and in addition, such a match would establish his claim to a share of their wealth. After all, Freydor too was a man of Ib.

So Freydor took the bodies from the casket and brought them to the bank of the river and buried the two passengers with all due rites under a ledge of red sandstone, said to be particularly favored by the dead on account of the fossils of ancient sea creatures it bore. The corpse lights continued to burn over the newly dug grave, so he knew that the rites he performed were acceptable to the dead, who would now rest quietly. Then he concealed the casket under a low hanging bush at the river's edge, and he returned home and called his three daughters to his side.

The first, Mathilda, was tall and pale and had hair the color of flax and cold, blue eyes under a noble, lofty brow. He held out to her a magnificent necklace of silver and diamonds. "Mathilda, this is your dowry. Remember that you are stately, you rise above your peers as an elm tree, yet you are graceful like the willow. Put on your blue gown, adorn yourself with this necklace, and prepare to meet your husband."

To the second, Nerita, voluptuous, green eyed, hair the color of burnished copper, he held out a torque of red gold threads, crusted with rubies and woven around a core of dark utta wood. "Nerita, this is your dowry. Know that you are lithe and supple like the river otter, and as cunning as the mink. Put on your green gown, adorn yourself with this torque, and prepare to meet your husband."

And to the third, Lirila, dark of skin, black eyed, and raven haired, he gave a necklace of onyx set in ebony and iron and hematite. "Lirila, this is your dowry. You are quiet and mindful, yet of the three you are the strongest for those very reasons. Put on your white gown and this necklace of nighted onyx and prepare to meet your husband."

Each of his daughters did as she was commanded, and then they stood before him, each of them more lovely than any other in Hyperborea. "Now, my daughters," Freydor said. "Come with me to the river. I will set you in a vessel and you will sail up the river that enters the great forbidden forest. See that you do not approach the bank, lest you be taken by a demon or a dragon or a troll, but sail straightway until you come to the settlement of your husbands, the men who crafted this vessel, and there will you live. You will know these men by the quality of their houses, the wood, and the iron, and the gold, and the great riches of their home."

And Freydor set a sail on the coffin and a rudder, and then he set his daughters within, and with the first light of the morning and a fair southern wind, they set sail against the current, and Freydor stood on the banks and watched as they disappeared out of his sight, and still he remained on the bank for a long while after. At last, Freydor felt a strange chill fall on his narrow shoulders, and he went silently to his workshop and busied himself with mending his nets. After all, Freydor was a man of Ib.

Mathilda, Nerita, and Lirila found a fair wind behind them, and so after three days they came at last to where the settlement of the three brothers lay, which they knew by virtue of the rich cloth of gold banners fluttering beside the landing and by the pylons topped with great wooden heads of dragons carved in the same fashion as those on either end of the coffin. And it was darkest night, so the sisters ran their boat against the bank and concealed it under a bush, and then they stole silently into the settlement and wondered at the great riches in the carven wood, the stone, and the banners that fluttered below golden lamps affixed to masts of iron.

The three sisters came at last to Baldry's workshop. Within, they found magnificent carvings of wood, figures of beasts and nymphs, angels and demons. Many of the figures were adorned with gilt, or with jewels of rare fire and color that lighted the workshop even in the darkness.

And in the center of the room, they found the figure of a woman carved of rowan wood, seated in an ivory chair, adorned with fine woven linen and crowned with a wreath of willow leaves fashioned from emerald and silver.

"Perhaps it is an image of the maker's goddess," Lirila said.

"Perhaps it is," Mathilda replied. "But this is a rare chance, and I will not let it pass. Would men of such great substance as these take a fisherman's daughter to wife?" And she took the crown from the statue and set it on her own brow. "Here I shall sit until the morning," she announced.

"This is not wise," Lirila warned her sister. "Soon enough the maker will learn the truth of it."

"The craftsman creates the image because he longs for the true. Let him make of it what he will," Mathilda replied.

So her sisters removed the statue to the forest and concealed it beside the boat.

Next they came upon Wulfstan's workshop, and they marveled at the fine furs and the heads of mighty beasts mounted upon the walls. The weapons of the hunt lay upon a table, a long bow and a heavy spear and a great sword. Nerita took up a fur of the lithe cemerr and stroked it against her cheek as they explored. And in the center of the workshop, they found the figure of a women, cleverly stitched together from silken soft hides and fabrics twisted so finely that the threads could not be seen, and this figure was crowned with the hair of the copper colored tira wolf, rarest of all predators. On her brow, she bore a circlet of rude, red hammered gold, set with uncut emeralds. Nerita nodded approval, took the circlet, and set it on her brow. "So it is here just as it was in the other room. Sisters, here I shall sit until the morning." And her sisters removed the figure of furs and hides and silks and concealed it beside the boat.

Lastly they came to Odduin's forge and kiln, the room smoky and dark, a ruddy warm glow filling the air. The walls were lined with weapons of black iron, and the tables laden with gold and silver, wrought in fine wires and in massive plates, and they found jewels, raw and cut, heaped into coffers.

And in the center of the room, they found a statue of a woman, cast of black iron, adorned with dark jewels, onyx and jet and ebony wood. On her dark brow, she wore a circlet of polished black dragonclaw, bearing a single large gem seemingly black, but bearing a red fire that flashed forth at certain angles. Lirila could not resist a smile as she took the circlet and set it on her own brow, where it fit comfortably, but then, ashamed of her boldness, she set the crown aside on a workbench.

"Here you shall sit, Lirila, until the morning," her sisters announced. And her sisters removed the iron figure and concealed it beside the boat.

Then they each returned to the seat each had claimed and remained there until the morning. But Lirila did not place the dragonclaw crown upon her brow.

The pleasures and horrors of Hyperborea may be more clearly illuminated than in other realms, the pain and the ecstasies may be more keenly felt than in more mundane districts, but this they have in common with those of the rest of the world—neither of them lasts forever.

Each of the brothers was astonished at the success he had had in conjuring his wife. Each of these women was more fair than he could have hoped for, and their transformation into beautiful, loving, devoted brides was more complete than any of them had dreamt possible. Even more felicitous, the three wives seemed much at ease with one another, and at this the brothers were most astonished, for had the nymphs of the well of Uldar not warned the brothers that the waters of the well, though they could bring life to mere clay, would also breed enmity and strife?

And so for a time and half a time, the brothers and their wives lived together in complete harmony and bliss. Yet as is the case with such matters, difficulties were bound to arise, and so they did, to the misfortune of all.

And it came about in this way.

Wulfstan it was who first saw the change. For copper-haired Nerita had decided to cut her hair, a custom of her and of her sisters from of old, for their hair grew exceedingly fast and thick, and in the warm months they would often trim their locks to a cooler length. This Nerita did, and upon walking into Wulfstan's workshop, the great hunter, stitching together a fine gown of cemerr trimmed silk, the which her husband intended to present her as a gift, she so surprised him that he drove his needle quite through his thumb.

Bellowing in surprise, his thumb in his mouth, Wulfstan gaped at his wife. "How has your hair come away, my love?" he asked her.

"My hair, my husband?"

"No pelt treated by my hand ever loses its fur, wife. I have seen the beast shed its fur in the warmth of the year, Nerita, but I made you with nothing but winter fur in its richest and fullest state. And see here! Your beautiful hair!"

Instantly Nerita saw that he did not approve, but she was as sinuous as the river otter, both in her limbs and with her tongue. She did not care much for the close examination Wulfstan seemed intent upon making of her, so before he could rise from his work table and approach her, she slipped from his grasp and raised her chin in delicate hurt and turned for the door, stopping only briefly to cast an offended look back at her husband, the first such look of its kind. "If you do not approve of me, you have only yourself to blame, for you yourself fashioned me."

"So I did," Wulfstan said doubtfully, rooted to the floor as she disappeared through the door.

At once, Nerita repented her words, but she did not reply.

Baldry set aside the sapphire adorned silver ring he was polishing, the which he intended to present his wife the next evening, and he examined her curiously as she stood in the doorway to his workshop, the bright sunlight framing her from behind and highlighting her flaxen hair, scintillating with the diamonds he had strung for her willow-green ribbons. At least, he admired what of her hair was left on her head, for, as had her sister, Mathilda had cut her hair short.

"I have seen the willow cast its leaves in the fall, but never in the summer, my love..."

Mathilda raised a golden eyebrow at her husband as a charming blush stole across her pale cheek. "What does my husband mean with this riddle?" she asked.

Baldry stood and crossed the floor to her, and took a shortened lock in his hand, twining it between his fingers lovingly, yet the look on his face was appraising, craftsmanlike. Unwilling to explain herself, she simply turned from Baldry and started for the house, casting but a single glance back at her husband as she said, "If you do not approve of me, you have only yourself to blame, for you yourself fashioned me."

"So I did," Baldry replied slowly.

And Mathilda repented her words, but she did not reply.

Lirila sat before her glass, considering the long black tresses that fell in waves about her shoulders and spilled wantonly down her dark throat and across her breast. When her husband Odduin had first found her in his workshop so many months ago, sitting in the very seat where he had left the iron likeness of a maiden, he believed that his project had succeeded beyond his hopes. Then he looked first into her eyes.

"Your glance is black as pitch, maiden," he had said, knowing well that now she heard his words with living ears. "And yet I do see the fire of the forge in them, burning even now. Will it ever be cooled?"

"It will not, my husband, so long as we love."

"How could I have hoped to have succeeded so wonderfully? Yet, there is more here than iron and clay, I think. I cannot forge a soul in that furnace," Odduin said. His face grew dark and grim. "And it is plain that you are a living soul. There is more here than my craft or the waters of the spring of Uldor."

She wondered if the ruse was a failure. She wanted to reveal the truth to him, willing to take the risk herself, yet she feared for her sisters, and as she was not quite sure what he did suppose her to be, she was afraid to ask.

Odduin drew near and reached out to touch her, his hand drawing near hesitantly, as if he still feared that the fires of her forging might burn within. Yet he found her dark smooth throat warm, her long black hair silken and soft.

Then he fell to his knees and plighted his troth to her that instant. When she received his pledge, he rose and placed the dragonclaw crown upon her head, bearing a single large black gem in the center that cast back no light except, at certain angles, a single flash of deepest garnet red. In placing that crown on her head, she felt a sudden horror, and she would have set the thing aside at once and told him all, but she did not. And she had carried this heavy secret in her heart, for in truth, she loved him well.

And so Lirila now sat before her mirror of polished crystal framed in gold, her silver shears in her hand, and she hesitated.

Her reverie was disturbed by the sound of agitated weeping outside her window, and she crossed the room to look out upon her sisters, wringing their hands upon the paving stones. Fetching them to a quiet grove, she heard their stories.

That night as she slept, Lirila was awakened by the sound of her husband's voice, conferring with his brothers. She recognized Wulfstan's strong grumbling words: " 'If you do not approve of me, you have only yourself to blame, for you yourself fashioned me.' That is what she said to me! This woman, divine in form and perfection—she blamed—me!"

"And so it was with Mathilda, just so!" Baldry said, his voice a sinister murmur. "And since then, she has not spoken to me. But Lirila, brother. What of her? Has she too shown any signs of corruption or defect?"

"She has not, nor would I believe that she could, for—for whatever she is, fairy or spirit, there is surely more in her than I could forge with my craft."

"Nonsense. They have said it themselves! She is your work, brother. As is mine and as is Baldry's. We fashioned them to perfection, and so they were perfect. Or, almost perfect. And this must be mended," Wulfstan said.

"And so it must," Baldry agreed. "For mine, a bonfire I think. And from the ashes of her burning I shall create again. I still have some drops of the waters of the spring of Uldor, and my first essay in this craft was so near to perfection. . . ."

"Then it is settled. Our craft is not perfected yet, not worthy of the great task we undertook. We shall begin again, and then we shall have all as it should be."

Lirila was not certain which brother spoke those last words, but she did not wait to inquire further.

She flew to her sisters' sides and drew them down to the riverside wherein they had concealed the effigies so many months ago. There they still lay, hidden in the tangled jasmine alongside the coffin.

"Now, sisters, all is lost. We must fly!"

"Have our husbands discovered our secret?" Mathilda asked, her cheek pale and wan.

Lirila laughed bitterly. "Would they had thought us goddesses, or fishermen's daughters! Our husbands have decided that they must repair their work, and they mean to begin by destroying us that they might create again. Let us replace these images in their workshops and get us gone before they destroy us in their desire to perfect us."

And so they did, but not a moment before time, for just as the first light appeared in the eastern sky, they heard a cry from Baldry's workshop, and then another from Wulfstan's, and at last, a cry from Odduin's forge, and they knew that the images had been discovered.

Lirila wondered at that cry, and she hesitated at the water's edge, but her sisters drew her toward the boat.

And with that, they betook them to the coffin, pushed it out into the current, and began the long journey south toward the evil city of Ib.

The three sisters tarried in Ib for a time and half a time, until even after they had brought forth the children of Odduin, Wulfstan, and Baldry.

Lirila made it her custom to walk along the bank of the great river with her child in the twilight. She was careful to stay clear of the forest, for she would not have her treasure stolen by demon or dragon or troll. She would admire his hair, dark and smooth and fine as if it were onyx spun on a loom of the gods, and his smooth cheek, polished like rosewood from the jungle forest of Umber, and his eyes, burning with the light of Odduin's forge. She wondered if that light would ever be cooled. But she knew it would not, not in this child. For she knew the forge wherein that light had been kindled, and it would never cool.

Yet still the three sisters delayed to return to their husbands, for they fretted about what defect their husbands might still find in their wives.

And the three brothers never repeated their experiment, and they crafted no other images, but rather they adorned the mute things that they had made with their own hands, and remained ever hopeful that one day, they might wake to life again.

But they did not wake to life again, and after a time, it became difficult to imagine that the three women they had fashioned had ever been otherwise.

At last there came a twilight when Lirila espied a craft sailing down the river, and she ran to the bank to see what it might be. She saw that the craft bore the hallmark of the three brothers in the magnificent carven dragon heads at the bow and stern and in the wonderful golden hasps and hinges and in the marvelous silken coverlet that lay over the three figures concealed there. Three corpse lights burned over the princely vessel, and she was filled with horror at the thought of what might lie within. But before she could arrive at the vessel's side, the priests of the lying god Yerolka, at their ritual ablutions in the river, took the vessel and made it fast to the shore and drew back the coverlet to reveal the three effigies the brothers had fashioned.

The priests at once proclaimed this a miracle, for had not the gods sent them their very own images to worship and adore, instead of the vain things before which they had until now prostrated themselves? So they took the images to the temple, cast down the image of Yerolka, and all Ib worshipped the three goddesses in the darkened temple, lit only by the corpse lights that refused to dim.

Lirila brought this news to her sisters at once.

"But what do the burning lights over the figures mean?" Mathilda asked. "That these figures truly lived, after all?"

"Yes, sister," Lirila said. "And ask yourself—what was it that brought life to the effigies?"

And the three sisters, knowing what this must mean, betook themselves to the boat and set sail with their children up the river.

But whether they arrived at last, and what they may have found there, or whether they were taken by a fiend as they sailed through the great forest, none could say. For none in Ib ever ventured into the great forest, knowing it to be the haunt of demons, dragons, and trolls.

About the story

With some stories, I can remember where I was standing when I got the idea. "The Three Sisters" didn't come to me quite so immediately, but seemed to slowly crystallize out of what I have learned from life with my wife and daughters, and about how difficult you can make things for yourself when you worry that you aren't seeing things the way they are. Still, that could be the origin of a lot of stories. The central image of the three women replacing the three brothers' icons with themselves seemed to spring full formed and armored into my head.

A question for the author

Q: What book or books inspired you as a child?

A: There are images in my mind, vague recollections of scenes and settings and disjointed plot fragments really, that I have carried along for as far as my memory goes back. I'm sure that most of them come from traditional fairy stories, Grimm's brothers, Hans Christian Anderson, Appalachian folk tales, and who knows what else. These images seem to be the foundation that underlies everything I write, and I can't even dredge up a recollection of where I got them. I wish I could, for I would love to go back and read them again, but I suspect that what they were wouldn't bear much resemblance to what they have become.

About the author

K.D. Azariah-Kribbs grew up in the hills of east Tennessee, a place where twilight starts early and lasts long. He studied geology in school, but when that didn't answer the big questions he went back for medieval English literature. That didn't quite do it, either. He traveled widely as a prospector, decided southern India has the best climate anywhere, and now writes speculative fiction in Maryland, where it's easy to speculate about how things might have been otherwise.

azariahkribbs.com